"No!" Ashleigh screamed, and jumped from her chair. She watched in horror as Aladdin stumbled to his knees, sending Rhoda flying over his shoulder.

The blood pounded in Ashleigh's ears, drowning out the gasps of the people around her as they watched the terrible spectacle below.

Rhoda tumbled beneath the hooves of Clever Patrol, while Aladdin slid along the ground on his side, his legs scrambling to get a foothold on the track.

Ashleigh's heart seemed to stop altogether as Aladdin came to a halt against the post of the inside rail, lying still for a moment before he floundered around, legs flailing in the air, and finally scrambled to his feet. He stood, momentarily stunned, then shook himself and took off at a gallop, heading for the track exit.

The next movement Ashleigh saw was the paramedics hopping the fence and sprinting over to the downed rider.

Was Rhoda all right? Was she dead?

Collect all the books in the Ashleigh series:

*Coming soon

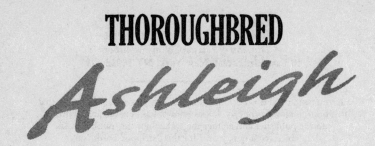

THOROUGHBRED

Ashleigh

DERBY DAY

CREATED BY

JOANNA CAMPBELL

WRITTEN BY

CHRIS PLATT

HarperEntertainment

A Division of HarperCollinsPublishers

HarperEntertainment
A Division of HarperCollins*Publishers*
10 East 53rd Street, New York, NY 10022-5299

Dedicated to Jan, Pat and Sarah, Billie, Rezalia, and Terri.
Thanks for being great friends. And to my editor, Cecily von Ziegesar,
for hanging in there and showing great patience.

Produced by 17th Street Productions,
a division of Daniel Weiss Associates, Inc.

ISBN 0–06–106606–0
HarperCollins®, ☰ ®, and HarperEntertainment™ are trademarks
of HarperCollins Publishers Inc.

Cover art © 1999 by Daniel Weiss Associates, Inc.

First printing: November 1999

Printed in the United States of America

Visit HarperEntertainment on the World Wide Web at
http://www.harpercollins.com

❖ 10 9 8 7 6 5 4 3 2 1

1

"How could they pick him to run dead last?" ten-year-old Ashleigh Griffen asked as she closed the *Daily Racing Form* in disgust. The family station wagon pulled out onto the main road, and Ashleigh stared out the car window as Edgardale, her home, with its two-story white farmhouse, large brown broodmare barn, and acres of rolling fields, got smaller and smaller.

The scenery passed by in a blur. Ashleigh's mind was set on the day's race and on Aladdin's Treasure, the Edgardale-bred colt who was going to run in it. This wasn't just any race. It was the Blue Grass Stakes, a high class race for three-year-olds, and one of the major stepping stones to the Kentucky Derby.

Of course, not all of the horses in the Blue Grass Stakes would enter the Derby. A horse had to be nominated into the Kentucky Derby when it was young, and a fee had to be paid annually to keep it eligible. If a nominated horse hadn't won any races or didn't perform well in the Derby prep races, including the Jim Beam Stakes, the Arkansas Derby, or the Blue Grass Stakes, it wasn't worth paying the final high entry fee to get into the Derby.

The Danworths, the rich Florida family who had purchased the black colt from the Griffens as a promising yearling, had nominated Aladdin for the Kentucky Derby as a show of faith. But Aladdin's career had gotten a rocky start, and so far he had won only one race. If he didn't do well in the Blue Grass, there was no chance they would send him to run in the Derby.

But it was still an honor to have an Edgardale-bred horse running in the Blue Grass Stakes. Ashleigh smiled to herself. She had told her chestnut mare, Stardust, all about it the night before, when she was cleaning her stall.

Ashleigh looked at the photo on the cover of the *Racing Form*. It was a picture of Star Gazer, the horse picked to win that day's Blue Grass Stakes, and the favorite for the Kentucky Derby. The photo showed only Star Gazer's fine bay head. *He's pretty,* Ashleigh thought. *But Aladdin can beat him. I know he can!*

Mrs. Griffen turned in the front seat and handed Ashleigh an old *Racing Form* with the results of some of Aladdin's previous races. "The *Racing Form* handicappers don't like Aladdin in this race, but you've got to remember that Aladdin has showed potential only in his last two starts," she said. Ashleigh's five-year-old brother, Rory, squirmed as their mother ran her hands through his red-gold hair, trying to tame the rooster tail that had popped up.

Ashleigh had her father's dark hair and hazel eyes, but her thirteen-year-old sister, Caroline, and Rory were both blond and blue-eyed like their mother. Mr. Griffen glanced into the rearview mirror as he spoke. "People are saying that Mr. Danworth is too optimistic about Aladdin. They don't think he belongs in this race." He turned the car onto Highway 60, heading toward the Keeneland racetrack. "We know that Aladdin is bred to run with the best of them, Ashleigh, but his performance record doesn't reflect that," her father continued.

Ashleigh hated to admit it, but her father was right. Aladdin had had seven starts as a three-year-old, but except for his last two successful races—one win and one second—he had never finished any closer than seventh. Most of the time he had been dead last.

The month before, the Danworths had invited Ashleigh's family to their big Thoroughbred farm in Florida. During that time the Griffens had tried to help Mike Smith, the Danworths' trainer, figure out why Aladdin was performing so poorly. Ashleigh was the one who had solved the mystery.

At the end of their stay, Ashleigh had blackmailed thirteen-year-old Peter Danworth into letting her ride Aladdin. The black colt had run away with her on the beach and tossed her into the sand, but the accident revealed the clue to Aladdin's poor performances. Aladdin's blinkers had fallen down onto his nose, and he ran like the wind. Ashleigh saw then that Aladdin needed a shadow-roll noseband to make him put his head down and flatten out his awkward gait. After the equipment change, the colt had won his next race and finished second in his last one. Ashleigh was convinced Aladdin was only just beginning a long and successful career.

Ashleigh opened the *Racing Form* again. She had to admit that she was a little worried about this race. This would be the first time that Aladdin would go up against horses of this caliber. In her heart she knew the colt had the ability to run with the best of them, but none of the handicappers had picked Aladdin even to place, let alone win. She supposed the handicappers were looking at Aladdin's five losing races.

"Who's Aladdin's jockey today?" Caroline asked, leaning forward to peer over her father's shoulder.

"Zach Jackson," Mr. Griffen answered. "He's riding Go for Cover for the Danworths in an earlier race, too."

"But why isn't Rhoda Kat riding Aladdin?" Ashleigh asked. "She knows how to make him win. The best Zach Jackson's ever gotten with him is second place."

Mr. Griffen smiled. "Rhoda would have been my first choice, too, but Mike says Mr. Danworth felt that Zach had done a good job and should be given another chance."

Ashleigh frowned. *Rhoda should be riding Aladdin today,* she thought.

"Here it is," Mrs. Griffen said as they turned off the freeway and onto the beautifully manicured grounds of Keeneland.

Ashleigh put away the racing paper and gazed out the window. She loved this track, with its lush green lawns, pines, oaks, and flowering pink and white trees. Keeneland was open year-round for training and for the public to come and enjoy. They even had a library.

Ashleigh scrambled out of the car as soon as it stopped. She took a deep breath, inhaling the wonderful smell of horses and crisp Kentucky air.

The Griffens waited at the back gate while the guard paged Mike Smith to come sign them into the stable area.

In a few minutes the trainer appeared around the corner of the barn, his smile widening when he saw them.

"Glad you could make it." Mike tipped his hat and brushed his hand through his steel-gray hair. "The Danworths won't be here for this race. Mr. D. had some problems with the builders on his new broodmare barn, so they'll be watching this one from home."

"Darn," Caroline said with a frown. "I was looking forward to seeing Peter again."

Ashleigh remained silent, but she was disappointed, too. She and Peter Danworth hadn't hit it off when they first met, but they had united to help Aladdin win his first race, and now they were friends.

"We're stabled in barn forty," Mike said as he led the way.

Ashleigh looked out across the immense stable yard. With forty-six barns of racing stock, Keeneland housed a lot of beautiful horses, and she intended to see every one of them.

Ashleigh moved Rory between her and Caroline so they could keep an eye on him. The races were just getting started, and there was a lot of activity, with grooms and trainers scurrying to and fro, trying to ready their horses.

Ashleigh marveled at how clean the stable area was and how each trainer displayed his or her stalls differently from the next. Some of the shed rows carried the trainer's stable colors, others had flowers and small bushes in the aisle, and at a few, expensive leather halters with brass nameplates hung outside each horse's door.

As they passed one of the stalls Ashleigh could hear the horse inside digging at his bedding. She stepped closer to peer in at the small bay horse that stood near the back wall. "This one seems pretty nervous," she said. "He's digging big holes in—"

In the next instant Ashleigh jumped backward as the little bay flew to the front of the stall and stretched his neck over the top of the door, baring his teeth at her and coming just inches from her chin.

"Whoa! What's up with him? I didn't do anything to him," Ashleigh gasped as she regained her footing and gave the stall a wide berth.

"That's Star Gazer," Mike said. "I should have warned you about him. He's a mean one. He hates everybody and everything. He's even tried to savage the horses he's raced against."

Ashleigh was surprised. She had expected Star Gazer to look different. He was a compact horse, much smaller than he'd looked in his picture—and definitely meaner.

"I've given Zach instructions to steer clear of Star Gazer in today's race," Mike said.

Ashleigh gulped. What if the horse tried to bite Aladdin while they were running?

They entered Mike's shed row. The tall black stallion heard the commotion and poked his head over the stall door, nickering a greeting.

Ashleigh rushed to Aladdin's stall. "How have you been, handsome?" She scratched the colt behind the ears, laughing when Aladdin nuzzled her pocket, searching for a treat. Ashleigh was pleased that he remembered the pieces of carrot she used to bring him as a yearling. "Is it okay if he has these before the race?" she asked Mike. Ashleigh knew that many trainers withheld all food and sometimes water for several hours before a race.

"Go right ahead," Mike said. "I don't think those few bits will slow him down any."

Everyone laughed.

Ashleigh ran her hand over Aladdin's sleek black coat, marveling at his race-hardened muscles and perfect conformation. His mane was cut short in racing style, but his tail was long and flowing. She lifted Rory up so he could pet Aladdin's head.

"He looks great," Mr. Griffen said. "How's he feeling today? Do you think he's up for such a hard race?"

"He's in great shape," Mike said as he took a leather halter off the door peg and slipped it over Aladdin's head. "But you're right, this will be Aladdin's toughest race to date."

Ashleigh set her mouth in a determined line.

"You'll show them all, won't you, boy?" she whispered to Aladdin as she ran a hand down his white blaze.

"My groom will be done with Go for Cover in a minute," Mike said. "We'll get Aladdin ready to go, then you folks can keep an eye on the big guy while I take that colt over for his race."

Mike and the groom set to work, and it wasn't long before they heard the gate call for the race.

"Time to go." Mike stepped out of the stall and took Go for Cover's reins from the groom. The colt was a tall gray, with speckled pink skin around his eyes and a pink nose. "Why don't you all watch this race from the trainer's stands on the backside here? I'll meet you back at the barn after the race."

The Griffens followed Mike to the track entrance, then found a place in the observation stands and waited for the race.

Keeneland had a mile-and-a-sixteenth dirt track with two starting chutes, one at the top of the home-stretch and one on the backside for the shorter races. On the inside of the dirt track was a seven-and-a-half-furlong turf course. Ashleigh knew from reading dozens of books on racing and stacks of *Racing Forms* that a furlong was an eighth of a mile.

The starting gate was close enough that she would be able to see each horse leap from the gate and battle for position. She loved hearing the riders shout to each other and their mounts as they drove the horses from the starting gate.

As the horses trotted past the trainer's stand, Mr. Griffen said, "Go for Cover looks pretty good."

Mrs. Griffen nodded in agreement. "Yes, but I heard Mike tell the pony boy that he was a handful. I guess they've been having some training problems with him. Mike said he's a bad actor."

The horses were loaded into the gate, and Ashleigh heard the gate man yell for the riders to get ready. A moment later the buzzer rang and the gate popped open, sending the horses racing down the backside. One horse broke slower than the rest, taking several strides before dropping his head to the ground and bucking as hard as he could.

"Oh, no!" Mrs. Griffen said. "It's Go for Cover!"

"Ride 'em, cowboy!" Rory hollered with a giggle, but stopped when Ashleigh shot him a dirty look.

Ashleigh held her breath as she watched Zach hang on for a couple of jumps before he was vaulted into the air and over the colt's head. He landed flat on his back and looked as though he'd had the wind knocked out of him.

One of the outriders galloped his horse forward and caught the bucking colt, quickly taking him off the racetrack before the horses circled around again.

The medical crew immediately jumped the fence

and ran toward the fallen jockey. Ashleigh saw Mike shoot across the path, beating the medics as he sprinted over to where Zach lie. Zach tried to get up, but the medics forced him to lie still until they checked him out. As soon as the race was over, an ambulance pulled out onto the track.

"I hope he's all right," Caroline said as they walked back to the barn to wait for Mike.

"Will he be able to ride Aladdin in the Blue Grass?" Ashleigh asked.

Mr. Griffen rubbed his chin. "It depends on whether or not he was injured. The track physician will have to give him permission to ride."

They entered the shed row, and the outrider showed up with Go for Cover a moment later. The groom removed his bridle and put him in crossties. Everyone was nervously silent. *What if Zach can't ride?* Ashleigh wondered. The Blue Grass was only a couple of races away. *Who will ride Aladdin?*

Several minutes later Mike entered the shed row at a jog. "Mr. D.'s going to have to get rid of this colt," he said in disgust. "We've put a lot of work into Go for Cover, and he's not improving. I don't like having a horse in my training stable who hurts riders."

"Is Zach okay?" Ashleigh inquired.

"He's doing all right, but he's kind of shaken up," Mike said. "The track physician won't allow him to ride the rest of his races today." He gazed into the concerned faces around him. "We've got to find another rider for Aladdin."

"What about Rhoda Kat?" Ashleigh said. "She doesn't have a mount until the tenth race."

"You read my mind," Mike said with a smile. "I've got to get up to the office and see if we can get her for Aladdin's race." He handed Ashleigh a leather halter with the Danworths' brass nameplate on it. "You can start grooming him if you like, Ashleigh."

"Thanks!" Ashleigh said, reaching for the halter. She slipped it on over the black colt's head, praying that Rhoda would agree to ride him.

Fifteen minutes later Mike returned, whistling a tune. "We got our girl," he said as he entered Aladdin's stall.

"Great!" Ashleigh couldn't keep the grin off her face. She felt bad for Zach, but she knew Aladdin liked Rhoda best and would give her everything he had. Together, Rhoda and Aladdin would prove those handicappers wrong!

"There's the first call for Aladdin's race," Mrs. Griffen said.

"Are you ready for the drench gun?" Mr. Griffen asked as he filled the large metal syringe with cool, clean water and handed it to the groom.

Mike grabbed the white leather bridle with the

thick fleece shadow roll and removed Aladdin's halter. Aladdin opened his mouth to accept the snaffle bit, eager to be off and running. Mike took the drench gun and inserted it between Aladdin's lips, washing bits of leftover hay and grain from the big colt's mouth.

"Looks like we're all set. All we need now is the call to the gate."

As soon as he said it, the pony horse came to the end of the shed row and the final call sounded. Ashleigh stepped back as the trainer led Aladdin from the stall and handed him off to the pony boy.

"Oh, before I forget, I've got something from Mr. Danworth for the soon-to-be birthday girl," Mike said. He pulled a pale blue envelope out of his jacket pocket and handed it to Ashleigh.

"For me?" Ashleigh said as she took the card from the trainer. Her birthday was in two weeks. It was nice of the Danworths to remember.

"It's not money, but it's something really special," Mike said. "I want you to wait until after the race to open it. The surprise might be even better by then." Mike smiled and gave her a wink.

Ashleigh handed the envelope to Caroline for safe-keeping. She didn't trust herself not to open it before she was supposed to.

Ashleigh fell into step behind Aladdin. It was finally

race time. She didn't care what the handicappers said, or how fast the other horses were—she knew Aladdin could win this race.

When they reached the front side, Ashleigh squeezed her way through the horse people and bettors crowded around the paddock. The saddling area could be seen from any one of the three floors of the grandstand, but she liked to be right down by the horses. Keeneland had sixteen saddling stalls, but there were only twelve horses running in the Blue Grass Stakes. Aladdin had drawn eighth position, and as she watched the colt waiting patiently to be saddled, Ashleigh drew in her breath. Aladdin looked great. His black coat gleamed, his muscles rippled, and his long tail almost swept the ground. He was the best-looking horse in the race.

There was a loud commotion from one of the first stalls, and Ashleigh turned to see Star Gazer kicking at the man trying to saddle him. Another loud bang filled the air as the colt's hoof slammed against the wall. Ashleigh was glad the rank colt wasn't near Aladdin.

She turned her attention back to Aladdin, who was dancing in place while the girth was tightened. Mike talked quietly to Rhoda, a petite dark-haired girl with a serious expression, giving her the race strategy for that day's run. Ashleigh smiled. Someday that was going to be her out there in jockey's silks!

The jockeys mounted up, and Ashleigh grabbed Rory and Caroline and ran to get a spot on the front fence so they could watch the horses in the post parade.

Star Gazer had the number 2 on his saddle cloth. The little bay colt nipped at his pony horse and kicked up his heels. Ashleigh hoped he stayed away from Aladdin during the race.

All of the horses in the post parade looked incredible. Ashleigh felt a small prick of doubt enter her thoughts as she watched them. These horses had won multiple stakes races. Some of them were even undefeated.

But when the stunning black colt pranced by with his neck bowed, chomping eagerly at the bit, Ashleigh's faith was renewed. Aladdin would give them all a run for their money!

"Uh-oh," Caroline said as she pointed to the tote board that displayed the odds. "Aladdin is forty to one. Those are pretty high odds."

Ashleigh frowned. Odds didn't mean everything. Aladdin's odds had been even worse when he had won his first race.

"Ashleigh, Caroline," Mrs. Griffen called, "we're going to watch the race from the clubhouse. Would you and Rory like to join us?"

Ashleigh motioned for Caroline to take Rory and

go with their parents. She hated to sit up in the club-house, far away from the horses. She wanted to stand as close as she could get.

Mike joined Ashleigh on the rail a moment later. "This is it, kid. Today we find out what kind of a horse we've really got."

Ashleigh stood on her toes to get a better view. Already the gate crew was loading the first horse into the starting gate. As they did, Star Gazer threw a tantrum, rearing high into the air and dragging his handlers around behind the gate.

"Will they load Star Gazer last since he's a problem horse?" Ashleigh asked.

Mike shook his head. "No, they can't in a stakes race. He has to be loaded according to his gate position."

The little bay colt entered the gate, but he immediately bounced against the front doors, shaking them noisily. Nervous whinnies floated back to the onlookers as the rest of the field was loaded in.

Ashleigh saw Aladdin's head lower and his front leg paw at the dirt. His gate handler jerked at his cheek strap, but it was too late. The starter pushed the button and the bell rang, sending the doors clanging open as the horses charged out of the gate.

Ashleigh's breath caught in her throat as she watched Aladdin lift his head in surprise. The big colt hesitated for a second, then sprang from the gate, his

16

powerful haunches straining as he stretched his legs, trying to catch up to the rest of the horses.

"Gallant Miss is in the lead, with Ruler's Pie running second and Handsome Gent coming in third," the announcer's voice boomed.

By the time they passed the grandstand and headed into the first turn, Aladdin was running in tenth place.

"Well, Aladdin used a lot of steam to catch them, but he looks like he's settled into his pace now and is running easy," Mike said, a hint of doubt in his voice.

Ashleigh lost sight of Aladdin as the horses came out of the first turn and headed up the far side of the track. "He's still running at the rear of the pack," Ashleigh said as the horses moved back into sight. "Is that where you told Rhoda to keep him?"

Mike tapped his racing program on the fence, his mouth turning down in a frown. "No, he's supposed to be sitting just off the leaders, ready to make a run for the lead in the homestretch."

Rhoda moved Aladdin past a few horses, but Aladdin was still running in the middle of the herd.

"Star Gazer is making his move on the inside. Gallant Miss has slipped back to third, and Ruler's Pie is now in the lead," the announcer said.

"Come on, Rhoda, get him up there," Mike urged from the fence, but Aladdin held his position in the middle of the field of twelve horses.

"As they come into the final turn, Made of Gold moves up to challenge the leaders. Star Gazer goes with him on the outside, and the front-runners are fading," boomed the announcer.

Ashleigh leaned over the fence, trying to see around the person beside her. "Aladdin's moved into fourth place," she yelled. "Why doesn't Rhoda go through the opening on the inside?"

At that moment Ashleigh saw a movement among the front-runners as Star Gazer homed in on the lead horse and lunged toward the colt, knocking him sideways as his body came into contact with Made of Gold. The first three horses bogged down on the rail as their jockeys attempted to realign the horses without losing too much momentum.

Rhoda swung Aladdin wide and made a run down the middle of the track. Several others horses went with him, but they couldn't match the black horse's strides.

"There's trouble on the inside rail!" the announcer called. "Aladdin's Treasure and Crystal Storm have made their move on the outside, passing the front-runners as they race down the homestretch!"

"Come on, Aladdin!" Ashleigh pounded on the rail as she jumped up and down. "Don't let Crystal Storm catch you!"

"It's Aladdin's Treasure opening his lead by three,

with Crystal Storm running second and Star Gazer moving up to challenge for third!"

"Go!" Mike hollered above the roar of the crowd, waving his arms in the air as if trying to push the big horse on.

The announcer made his final call. "At the wire, it's Aladdin's Treasure by five lengths, Crystal Storm running second, and Star Gazer third." A few moments later the man's voice crackled across the PA system once again. "Ladies and gentlemen, please hold all tickets. There was some bumping in this race, and the stewards have posted an inquiry."

Ashleigh's heart fell. There was usually a little bumping in every race. But when the interference was bad enough that track officials posted an inquiry, somebody usually got disqualified. "They won't take our number down, will they?" she said, glancing nervously at the tote board, where the race results were posted.

"They shouldn't touch us," Mike said. "We weren't part of that fiasco. But you never know."

Aladdin trotted up to the rail. His eyes were caked with track dirt and his nostrils were extended. Rhoda walked him a circle, flagging her whip up toward the stewards' box to show that she called no fouls for the race.

Rhoda smiled at Ashleigh from Aladdin's back. "We

had a clean ride, Ashleigh," she called. "We won that race fair and square."

As if to back up the jockey's words, the official race results were posted and a cheer went up from the crowd as Aladdin's number stayed in first place. There was some grumbling from the bettors as Star Gazer's number was removed from the board.

"Aladdin, with twenty-year-old Rhoda Kat aboard, has won this year's running of the Blue Grass Stakes," the announcer called.

"Yes!" Ashleigh screamed as she slapped Mike a high five. Aladdin had just beaten a whole field of Derby hopefuls!

Ashleigh's family piled down the grandstand steps and followed Mike and Ashleigh to meet Aladdin and Rhoda in the winner's circle.

Aladdin stood proudly for the win photo, with Rhoda beaming from his back.

"I think now would be a good time to open that birthday card," Mike said, turning to Ashleigh. "It just gained a lot of value."

Ashleigh was so excited about Aladdin's race, she almost dropped the card when Caroline handed it to her. She opened it, wondering what could possibly make it more valuable now than it had been before the race. Five pieces of paper floated to the ground.

"They're tickets," Ashleigh said in surprise as she

knelt beside Rory to pick them up. She looked more closely at the print, then let out a whoop as she jumped to her feet. "Tickets to the Kentucky Derby! One for each of us!" Ashleigh cried.

"That's Mr. Danworth's way of saying thank you," Mike said with a smile. "Aladdin wouldn't be winning if it weren't for you."

Ashleigh handed the tickets to her mother. She didn't want to chance losing something so special. Then she turned to Mike. "But I don't understand. Why are the tickets more valuable now than before the race?"

"That's the best part," Mike said with a grin. "I spoke to Mr. Danworth this morning. You know he's always had high hopes for Aladdin. He decided that if Aladdin ran well today, he was going to pay the entry fees and run him in the Kentucky Derby."

There was a moment of stunned silence, then chaos broke loose as everyone spoke at once.

"The Derby!" Ashleigh's parents chorused.

Ashleigh laughed at how excited they looked— almost as excited as she felt. At last Edgardale was going to have a Derby horse!

2

"Everyone look here for the win photo," the track photographer instructed.

"I knew you could do it!" Ashleigh said as she smiled up at Rhoda.

The jockey removed her helmet and grinned at Ashleigh, then sat up straight and pulled Aladdin's head around for the picture. When the photos were done, Rhoda hopped down and removed her saddle for the weigh-in.

Mike pulled the reins over Aladdin's head. "Come see me at the barn after the races," he said to Rhoda. "I want to talk to you about riding Aladdin in the Derby. Are you interested?"

"You bet she is!" Ashleigh said, then gasped, her cheeks turning hot as she realized she had completely overstepped her bounds.

Ashleigh let out her breath when everyone laughed and Rhoda clapped her on the back.

"I couldn't have said it better myself." Rhoda grinned, then turned to Mike. "I'll come by later and we'll work out the details."

Mrs. Griffen tugged on Ashleigh's arm. "Come on, Ashleigh. Let's run on ahead and help the groom get Aladdin ready to go to the test barn."

Ashleigh nodded. Now that Aladdin had won the race, he would have to go straight to the test barn. Winning horses, or favorites that ran poorly, had to be tested to make sure they weren't running on illegal drugs. If any drugs were detected in Aladdin's sample, he would be disqualified from the race and the purse would be redistributed to the other placing horses.

Ashleigh hurried along beside her mother. She glanced back to see how Aladdin was doing and smiled proudly. His head was up and his ears were pricked alertly. Everyone had said that Aladdin had no business being in this race, but he had beaten all the other horses, and he didn't even look tired.

Ashleigh slowed down as they approached the horses and owners walking in front of them.

"It's a crying shame," the tall, skinny man walking Made of Gold, a bright chestnut, said. "That black colt had no business running with this class of horses." He spit a stream of tobacco juice onto the dirt track. "If it

23

hadn't been for Vargas's crazy colt trying to take a bite out of Gold's hide and knocking all the favorites out of this race, that Aladdin horse wouldn't have gotten any part of it!"

Ashleigh stopped in her tracks, glancing at her mother to see if she had heard. Her mother gave her a look that said it would be better to keep quiet at that moment. Ashleigh felt weak in the knees. What did he mean, Aladdin wouldn't have had any part of it?

Another trainer with a prancing chestnut horse passed by as they exited the track into the barn area, and Ashleigh overheard him say, "My horse should have won that race. Whoever heard of Aladdin's Treasure? That horse hasn't won but one race in his entire life, and it wasn't even a big stakes race."

Ashleigh suddenly felt as though she'd just done a belly flop off a high diving board. *What are they talking about?* she asked herself. Aladdin had run a great race. Why were they trying to take that away from him?

"It's okay, Ash." Mrs. Griffen patted Ashleigh's shoulder. "Some people don't take losing very well."

Ashleigh focused on her mother's sympathetic gaze. "He ran a good race, didn't he?"

Mrs. Griffen steered Ashleigh past the trainers and hurried her along. "He didn't run a good race, Ash. He ran a *great* race. And he won!"

Ashleigh smiled. "Yeah. He won," she repeated for her own benefit. They entered the barn, and she ran to gather the buckets and things they'd need at the test barn.

Mike was just bringing Aladdin to the wash rack when they entered the test barn gate. Ashleigh laughed as the big horse craned his neck, trying to get a drink from the hose.

Mike held Aladdin while the groom scraped the excess water from Aladdin's damp coat. "Bring me that water bucket, will you, Ashleigh?" Mike asked.

Ashleigh held the water bucket as Aladdin drank. His kind eyes stared into hers. "I don't care what they say," she whispered. "I know you're a champion. You'll beat them again in the Derby."

The Kentucky Derby! She couldn't wait to get home and tell Stardust that one of Edgardale's horses was going to the Derby! And she'd have to call her best friend, Mona Gardener, as soon as possible and tell her the news. Maybe her parents could get another ticket so that Mona could go, too.

The Derby was always run on the first Saturday in May. That meant they had three weeks left to get ready. And Ashleigh's eleventh birthday was only two weeks away. This was going to be the best birthday ever!

When they finished up at the test barn, Mr. Griffen walked Aladdin back to the barn while Mike went to see how Zach was doing. Rhoda was waiting at the barn when they arrived.

"Hey there," the jockey said as she hopped off the stack of straw bales she was perched on. "They scratched my mount in the tenth race, so I thought I'd come by the stable before everyone went home for the night. Is Mike still here?"

"Mike went to see about Zach," Mr. Griffen said as he stepped forward and extended his hand to shake Rhoda's. "You rode a great race!"

Mrs. Griffen smiled. "You were terrific out there, Rhoda. A lot of people didn't think Aladdin had a chance. You proved them all wrong."

Rhoda nodded and smiled her thanks, then turned to look at Ashleigh. "I hear there's at least one person who knew we could do it."

Ashleigh stood up a little straighter, pleased to be singled out by the jockey. "I knew you'd win," she said. "You're one of the best riders here. Someday I'm going to be a jockey, and I want to be just like you." Ashleigh felt the color rise to her cheeks. *Rhoda probably thinks I'm crazy,* she thought. But the jockey reached out and placed a hand on her shoulder.

"Thanks. I'm flattered," Rhoda said, smiling. She leaned back against Aladdin's door and hitched her thumbs into her belt loops. "I think it's great that you want to be a jockey. We need more women riders out there to keep the guys in line," she joked. "And Mike told me he thought you had a lot of potential. I'll be looking forward to a little friendly competition in a couple of years."

Ashleigh blushed, unable to hide her pleasure at the jockey's words.

Mike walked up the shed row. "They say Zach's all right. They've released him to ride in tomorrow's races."

Everyone breathed a sigh of relief. Horse racing was a dangerous sport, and often a jockey's career was cut short by a fall like the one Zach had taken that day. He was lucky not to have any broken bones.

"Well, do you think you can handle this big fella for the Derby?" Mike said to Rhoda as he grabbed Aladdin by the halter and patted him fondly.

"I'll give it my very best," Rhoda promised. "What's his work schedule going to be? Will Aladdin be staying here at Keeneland or going to Churchill Downs to train?"

Mike removed Aladdin's halter and signaled for the groom to bring over the hay net. "Mr. Danworth said he'd like to keep the colt in training here at Keeneland. We'll move him to Churchill Downs the week before the race."

"It sounds like a good plan," Rhoda said. "I'll be staying here at Keeneland myself. When do you want to gallop Aladdin next?"

Mike walked to the tack room to look at the calendar. "Well, he deserves a few days off after today's race. The front office has asked me to gallop him for the Saturday crowd at Breakfast with the Works next week. It's a big attraction for the fans when they get to see a Derby entry show off."

Ashleigh could hardly contain herself. Breakfast with the Works was one of her favorite things to do at Keeneland. On weekends during the race meet, you could eat a buffet breakfast in the Equestrian Dining Room, overlooking the racetrack, while a commentator gave a description of how each horse was working. And they were going to announce that Aladdin was a Derby horse!

Ashleigh looked pleadingly at her parents. They just had to take her.

"I know where Ash wants to have her birthday breakfast," Caroline teased as she nudged Ashleigh with her shoulder.

"At the hamburger place?" Rory said hopefully.

Mr. Griffen laughed and pulled Rory next to him. "No, silly, that's where we go on *your* birthday."

"Can we please go?" Ashleigh begged. "I know it'll be a week ahead of my birthday, but can't we do it early this year?"

Mrs. Griffen put her arm around Ashleigh and said, "Of course we can. It isn't every day that we've got a horse prepping for the Kentucky Derby.

Ashleigh hugged her parents. "Thanks. You're the best!"

As soon as Aladdin was settled in for the night, the Griffens left for home. When they reached Edgardale, the mares and foals in the front paddock trotted along the fence line as the Griffens' car turned down the long drive.

"There's Go Gen," Ashleigh said, pointing to Aladdin's dam. The gray mare trotted toward the barn with her new filly running beside her. Shadow, as they had named the black filly with the three white socks and a blaze, was a full sister to Aladdin and a half sister to Wanderer's Quest, another one of Edgardale's fillies that had won a lot of stakes races.

Ashleigh wished they didn't have to sell their yearlings, but that was how Edgardale made its money. Still, Ashleigh wished they could keep a few of them to run themselves.

Ashleigh watched Shadow run beside her mother. She looked so much like Aladdin, there could be no doubt that they were brother and sister. Ashleigh hoped the filly would follow in her big brother's footsteps. Only three fillies had ever won the Kentucky Derby in all the years it had been run. Maybe Shadow would grow up to join their ranks.

"I hope that someday Shadow will run in the Kentucky Derby," Ashleigh commented.

"Well, let's not get ahead of ourselves," Mr. Griffen said. "But having Aladdin in the Derby will definitely be good for business for Edgardale."

Mrs. Griffen nodded in agreement. "If Aladdin does well in the Derby, people will start to pay more for our yearlings."

Ashleigh sat as far forward as her seatbelt would allow. "Mr. Danworth promised that when Aladdin retired from racing, he'd stand him at stud here at home. If Aladdin wins the Derby, a lot of owners will want to bring their broodmares to Edgardale!" Ashleigh smiled. *Maybe then we'll have enough money to build a track and train our own stock,* she thought dreamily.

Mr. Griffen pulled their car to a stop in front of the old white farmhouse. "Let's change out of our good clothes and get down to the barn to help Jonas with the chores," he said.

Ashleigh ran up to her room to change. She couldn't wait to see Stardust. She liked to tell Stardust how her day had gone while she groomed and fed her, and so many wonderful things had happened.

Jonas, Edgardale's only hired hand, had already filled the hay nets and was mixing grain when Ashleigh arrived at the barn. "You can help your mother and father bring the mares and foals in," he said as he pointed to the halters and lead ropes that hung on the wall by the barn door.

Caroline and Rory helped with the feeding, while Ashleigh joined her parents in the paddocks. Soon they had everyone settled in, and it was time to fix their own dinner.

That night as Ashleigh got into bed she rehashed all the thrilling events of the day. Mona was away at her cousin's that weekend, but the two girls had planned to ride together after school on Monday. Ashleigh had so much to tell Mona—it would have to be a long ride!

The weekend passed too quickly for Ashleigh, and before she knew it, she was sitting at her desk in English class, daydreaming about Aladdin.

Ashleigh was supposed to be following along with a story her classmates were reading, but she couldn't keep her mind on the subject. Not when there were more exciting things to think about, such as the Kentucky Derby.

"Ashleigh?" The teacher interrupted Ashleigh's thoughts.

Ashleigh could tell by the tone of the teacher's voice that it wasn't the first time she had called her name.

"Yes, Mrs. Summers?" Ashleigh said as she sat up straighter in her chair, trying to ignore the giggles of her classmates.

Mrs. Summers arched a brow and stared at

Ashleigh over the rims of her glasses. "I asked if you would please finish reading where we left off."

Ashleigh felt a streak of dread race through her. She had no idea where the last reader had stopped. She glanced down at her open book, wondering if she was even on the right page. The girl at the next desk tilted her book so Ashleigh could see what page they were on. Ashleigh smiled at her gratefully.

"Go ahead," the teacher prodded.

Ashleigh's eyes raced over the page as she tried to find her starting place, her cheeks growing hot when she heard more laughter. She glanced at the girl who had helped her before and saw that she was tapping her finger at the top of page eight.

Ashleigh took a deep breath and began to read, but she couldn't block out her classmates' chuckling or the smirks on some of their faces. She stammered several times but forged ahead, trying to get through it so the teacher would move on to the next student.

Suddenly the whole class laughed, and Ashleigh realized that she must have pronounced something really wrong or spoken words that weren't even on the page. She glanced at her friends Mona and Lynne, who were seated in the back corner, and the look of sympathy on their faces told Ashleigh all she needed to know. She had really blown it.

"Now, class." The teacher banged on her desk, trying to get their attention. "Everyone makes mistakes. Let's settle down and let Ashleigh finish reading."

Ashleigh looked around the classroom. She knew that most of these kids weren't trying to be mean, but it still hurt. She didn't like being laughed at. Her face was growing hotter and hotter.

When the laughter calmed down a bit, Mrs. Summers continued. "Ashleigh, would you please finish reading to the bottom of the page?"

"Yeah, Ashleigh, that was pretty funny," the boy in the blue shirt sitting behind her whispered. The other students heard him, and the laughter started again.

Why did they keep laughing? She couldn't help it if she made a mistake. Ashleigh couldn't stand it any longer. She jumped up, and her book hit the floor.

"Ashleigh, are you all right? Where are you going?" Mrs. Summers asked. "Come back here."

But Ashleigh was already out the classroom door. She didn't want to disobey Mrs. Summers, but she was too embarrassed to stay in class. She was probably going to get in a lot of trouble for this, but all she wanted to do just then was to go home and be with her horse.

3

"It was awful!" Ashleigh said to Mona as she turned Stardust onto a familiar trail. "The whole class was laughing at me."

Mona directed her bay Thoroughbred mare down the same dirt path. A frown settled heavily between her brows. "I know," she said. "But don't worry. You get really good grades in English, Ash. Just because you get nervous reading in front of the class doesn't give them the right to make fun of you."

The passage Ashleigh had been asked to read was something about President Kennedy. Mona had explained that she'd said Aladdin's name instead of the president's.

Ashleigh reined Stardust toward the big field that bordered the back edge of Edgardale. She was glad Mona was able to ride that evening. She needed somebody to talk to. Her parents hadn't been very happy when the principal called to tell them what she had done. They had given her a long lecture about paying attention in class and obeying the teacher. They were sympathetic about her being laughed at, but they said she couldn't always run away from her problems.

But at the moment that was exactly what Ashleigh wanted to do—to turn Stardust loose and race as fast as she could through the knee-deep grass in the field they were heading toward.

"I was daydreaming about Aladdin, and I wasn't paying attention," Ashleigh told Mona. "I guess I sounded pretty dumb."

"It wasn't that bad," Mona reassured her.

Ashleigh's stomach did flip-flops as she remembered the smirking faces of her classmates. "All I could think about was getting out of that classroom." She reached down to stroke Stardust's neck, feeling the burn of embarrassment color her cheeks once again.

Mona urged Frisky up beside Stardust. "They'll forget all about it by tomorrow, Ash." She gave her friend a smile. "It's not like they all haven't made mistakes before."

"I know," Ashleigh said as she lifted her face to the cooling breeze. "Some kids even said they were sorry, but I don't think I can ever read out loud again."

They came into the clearing at the edge of Edgardale's land. Ahead of them lay miles of forest trails and a huge meadow with a few oak trees and a stream winding through it.

Ashleigh stopped and let Stardust put her head down to graze. People had always told her that she shouldn't let her mare eat while they were riding, but Ashleigh liked to give her horse a break. As long as she stretched her muzzle to the ground only when Ashleigh said it was okay, there wouldn't be a problem.

"Maybe you'll get lucky and Mrs. Summers won't ask you to read again for a while," Mona said.

Ashleigh felt her stomach tighten. "But what about our oral report?" She grimaced. The previous week Mrs. Summers had assigned a five-minute oral report on the topic of their choice. The written outline was due in a week, and they had to give the report a week after that.

"I forgot about that!" Mona said. "I wish I could help, but I'm not very good at speaking in front of the class, either. One thing's for sure," Mona added with a giggle. "You'd better think of something, because you can't keep running out of the classroom."

Ashleigh laughed in spite of herself.

"Don't worry about it, Ash," Mona said. "You'll do fine. Everyone gets nervous when they speak in front of crowds."

Ashleigh shifted in her saddle and stared out over the meadow to where the green Kentucky bluegrass met the blue of the springtime sky. She just wanted to race Stardust across the field, going so fast that all the terrible memories of her classmates' laughter would fade.

Ashleigh pulled Stardust's head up and squeezed her legs urgently against the mare's sides. Stardust jumped to attention and bolted off across the meadow.

"Let's race!" Ashleigh called back over her shoulder as she leaned low over her mare's withers and clucked. The little chestnut responded with more speed. *Who cares if they laughed at me?* Ashleigh thought as the wind whipped her face, bringing tears to her eyes. She pumped her hands up and down Stardust's neck, asking for more speed.

Ashleigh loved the feel of the wind in her hair as she drove Stardust on, going faster and faster. *This is what it must feel like to be a jockey,* she thought. She glanced back to see if Mona was catching up to her. She knew that Frisky, a full Thoroughbred, could outrun Stardust, but there would be a few seconds when the two mares would race neck and neck and it would feel just like riding in a race.

Ashleigh looked back again to see how close Mona was getting, and was surprised to see her friend galloping across the field, waving her arm in the air. She could hear the faint sound of Mona calling to her, but she couldn't hear her words.

What's wrong with Mona? Ashleigh wondered. She saw her friend pointing in the direction she was galloping, and Ashleigh turned to look where she was going. Her heart skipped a beat. She had forgotten about the creek, and now it loomed in front of her. It was too late to pull up.

How could she have forgotten about Jessica's Jump? Ten feet across and five feet down to the water, it had been named Jessica's Jump because of a young girl who had taken a dare and attempted to jump the creek. The horse hadn't made it across—he had to be put down—and Jessica had ended up in the hospital.

Ashleigh stood in the stirrups, as she had seen the jockeys do at the racetrack. She hauled back on the bit with all her might, but Stardust had racing on her mind and didn't want to slow down; especially with Mona and Frisky coming up behind them.

Ten feet across and five feet down. The blood ran cold in her veins as Ashleigh tried once again to slow Stardust. The wind stung her face, causing her eyes to water and making it difficult to see.

"Turn her, Ashleigh. Turn her!" Mona yelled as she pulled up her mare.

Ashleigh heard her friend, but her mind was working in slow motion. The creek was getting closer with every stride Stardust took. This couldn't be happening! Ashleigh seesawed on the reins, but Stardust's legs pumped like iron pistons as they ate up the ground beneath her hooves.

They were so close now that Ashleigh could see where the tall grass ended, signaling the edge of the creek. It seemed a long way across to where the grass began again on the other side.

"Turn her, Ashleigh!"

Mona's words finally cut through Ashleigh's muddled brain. She knew she couldn't stop Stardust, and she knew they couldn't make it over the creek.

Ashleigh put both hands on the left rein. There was so much adrenaline running through her body that her fingers were numb. She forced them to grip the rein.

They were practically on top of the creek now. Ashleigh stood in the stirrups and hauled back on the left rein with all her might. Stardust popped her head in the air, fighting against the bit. But Ashleigh sat back, putting all her weight into the half-inch leather strap, until the mare's dainty nose finally tipped to the left. Stardust snorted, but she had no choice other than to follow the way her nose was pointing.

With less than fifteen yards to go, Ashleigh pulled the mare in a big arc, bracing herself as she saw Mona cut Frisky onto Stardust's path in an attempt to slow them down.

Ashleigh swallowed the lump in her throat and jammed her feet forward in the stirrups as Stardust slammed on the brakes like a professional reining horse. Ashleigh hit the saddle hard three times before they came to a complete stop.

"Ashleigh, are you all right?" Mona said as she jumped off Frisky and ran to Ashleigh's side. "Did you forget the creek was there, or was Stardust running away with you?"

Ashleigh tried to quiet her shaking hands, but she couldn't hide the tremor in her voice. "I just wanted to run," she mumbled, looking back over her shoulder at the danger she had barely escaped. She dismounted, almost falling when her legs threatened to buckle beneath her as her feet touched the ground. She walked to the edge of the creek to peer down at the shallow stream of water that ran below.

Ashleigh couldn't believe that she had forgotten about Jessica's Jump. It had been the only thing the kids at school had talked about the previous year.

Poor Jessica Stanberg was in the same grade as Caroline. She had been a really good jumper. When her champion horse had begun refusing jumps, Jessica had given in to the teasing of a jealous girl and attempted to jump the creek at its widest part. It was the one jump her horse *should* have refused. The horse had broken its leg, and there had been nothing the vet could do. Jessica herself still had a limp.

Ashleigh ran a hand over her damp brow, grateful that Mona had warned her in time. She mounted up on Stardust, promising herself to start paying closer attention to things. Her wandering mind was beginning to get her in a lot of trouble.

They turned their horses to walk back toward Edgardale. Ashleigh had to make sure Stardust was cooled out and calm before they reached her home. She was in enough trouble as it was—she didn't want to have to tell her parents about what had just happened. She hoped her hands would stop shaking before she reached Edgardale.

The rest of the week dragged by like a month of Mondays. Ashleigh went about her normal routine of going to school, cleaning stalls, riding Stardust, and helping her parents and Jonas with the new foals. She and Mona went riding and did homework together after school, but it seemed as though nothing could speed up the time until she would get to see Aladdin.

Mike called midweek to tell them that Aladdin would be given a strong gallop on Friday so that he would be easier to handle when he was presented for the Saturday gallop at Breakfast with the Works.

Ashleigh had hoped that they were going to breeze

Aladdin so the crowd could see how fast he could go, but Mike didn't want to do any speed work with the colt until the following week. Aladdin had to be trained just right so that he would be in peak condition for the Kentucky Derby.

When Saturday finally came, Ashleigh was up at the crack of dawn. She quickly put on her clothes and ran down to the barn. She had just enough time to brush Stardust and help Jonas put the broodmares and foals out before it was time to leave for Keeneland.

She snapped Stardust into the crossties and picked up the rubber curry comb, running it in circles over her coppery coat. Stardust worked her lips, twisting them around when Ashleigh hit a spot that she liked.

Ashleigh laughed. "Silly. Do you know how funny you look?" she told the mare. When the mare's coat was shiny and clean, Ashleigh turned Stardust out in the back paddock and helped Jonas with the other horses. It wasn't long before it was time to leave.

On the way to Keeneland, Ashleigh studied a stack of new horse magazines. The Kentucky Derby was now two weeks away, and the *Daily Racing Form* had a lot of articles on the Derby entries. Star Gazer was still the Derby favorite, even after his dangerous performance in the Blue Grass.

Ashleigh had read that the ornery colt would be required to work out of the gate in front of the stewards to prove that he could race without biting the other horses. If he didn't pass the test, he wouldn't be allowed to race in the Kentucky Derby.

Ashleigh frowned. Aladdin would have beaten that colt even if Star Gazer hadn't wasted time trying to savage the other horses. Those owners and trainers would have to take back their hasty words when Aladdin was standing in the winner's circle at Churchill Downs!

"Here we are," Mr. Griffen said as he pulled the car into the valet parking area.

"First class all the way," her mother said with a smile.

"Thanks." Ashleigh grinned as she stepped out of the car. It was fun getting one of her birthday presents early—stretching out the celebration.

They made their way to the Equestrian Dining Room and got a table, then stood in line for the buffet. Everyone heaped their plates high with scrambled eggs, fried potatoes, pancakes, and a mix of fruits, but Ashleigh wasn't sure she would be able to eat much. She was too excited to have an appetite.

When their plates were as full as they could get, everyone sat down to enjoy the meal and watch the horses on the track below. For the next hour and a half they would listen to the announcer call the name of each horse that entered the track, and comment on how the horse was going. And Aladdin was going to be the star of the morning's workouts!

"If you'll turn your attention to the backside of the track, you'll see Blue Rain, a five-year-old stakes horse, stepping onto the track for his half-mile workout," the commentator said.

Ashleigh listened as the man went through a list of the horse's accomplishments and gave the time of each quarter split as the horse pounded around the track. While she was listening to the man speak, she kept her eyes glued to the back entrance to the track, waiting for Aladdin to make his appearance. She had just popped a piece of watermelon into her mouth when her father gestured with his fork, pointing toward the opposite side of the track.

"There he is," Mr. Griffen said, just as the commentator announced Aladdin's presence.

Ashleigh saw Mike lead Aladdin to the gate, then take a place on the outside rail.

"We have a special appearance by a Kentucky Derby entry this morning." The announcer spoke amid applause from the diners. "Aladdin's Treasure, winner of this year's Blue Grass Stakes, will be galloping this morning. His jockey, Rhoda Kat, will backtrack the colt past our grandstand so everyone can have a good look at him, then he'll remain in the middle of the track for an easy gallop.

"Just stepping onto the track is Clever Patrol, a two-year-old doing his first timed workout," the announcer continued. "Keep your eyes open for this one. Clever Patrol is a half brother to the Derby favorite, Star Gazer. This colt shows a lot of promise."

Mrs. Griffen wiped a spot of ketchup off Rory's cheek and handed Caroline the pitcher of orange juice. "Clever Patrol went through last year's sale with some of our yearlings," she said. "He brought a pretty high price."

Ashleigh took her eyes off Aladdin and Rhoda for a moment to watch Star Gazer's half brother. The chestnut colt entered the track prancing and tossing his head. His rider reined him in and warned the excited colt with a tap from the whip, but the colt only bucked and broke into a trot.

"I hope he has better manners than Star Gazer," Ashleigh said. But from the way the colt was nipping at the pony horse and pinning his ears, he didn't appear to be very well behaved.

Ashleigh turned her attention to Aladdin, who was parading in front of the grandstand. The big black colt bowed his neck and swished his tail, eager to be off. Rhoda turned him toward the inside rail, then trotted him around the track. After a few hundred feet he stepped up to a slow canter.

"What a good-looking colt!" someone said loudly.

Ashleigh smiled with pride as she listened to the praise coming from the other racehorse enthusiasts. A couple of weeks earlier hardly anybody had known who Aladdin was.

"He looks like he'd rather be going a lot faster," Mr. Griffen said as he helped himself to a waffle that Ashleigh couldn't finish.

Ashleigh watched Aladdin's progress around the track. Rhoda kept a tight hold on him, but Ashleigh could tell Aladdin was fighting the bit, eager to run faster.

The announcer's voice broke Ashleigh's concentration.

"Aladdin's Treasure has won two of his last three starts for his owner, Peter Danworth, of Hialeah, Florida," he said. "Aladdin is a Kentucky-bred horse raised a short distance from here at Edgardale Farm."

"That's us!" Ashleigh cried. Caroline grinned and slapped her a high five.

"Clever Patrol has settled down to work on the inside rail," the commentator said. "Aladdin is rounding the top turn and still moving nicely down the track."

Ashleigh watched Aladdin toss his head and strain at the bit. She wondered if Rhoda would be able to hold him when the red colt breezed by on the inside rail. Aladdin looked ready for a race that morning.

Ashleigh heard a gasp from the crowd and quickly scanned the track for signs of trouble.

"Clever Patrol has blown the turn, bolting from the inside rail to the outside of the racecourse!" the announcer called.

Ashleigh could see the colt's jockey standing in his stirrups, trying to pull the horse back down to the inside rail. She looked ahead to where Aladdin was galloping. Rhoda already had her hands full. Fast-working horses were supposed to stay on the inside rail—that was what everyone was used to. If Clever Patrol flew past Aladdin on the outside rail, Rhoda might not be able to hold him any longer.

"Come on, get him under control," Ashleigh whispered under her breath, but the two-year-old colt stayed where he was in the middle of the track.

Ashleigh saw Rhoda look back over her shoulder as the other horse and rider approached. In the next moment Clever Patrol flew past Aladdin on the outside. Aladdin pinned his ears and threw his head into the air, sitting Rhoda back down in the saddle. Aladdin had the bit in his teeth and was off and running.

Aladdin quickly caught up to Clever Patrol, running with him for the sheer joy of racing. Rhoda stood in the irons, hauling back on the bit as she tried to slow his pace. The horses flew down the stretch, neck and neck.

As they crossed the finish line Ashleigh could see that the red horse was tired. His head bobbed up and down and he lugged in on Aladdin, slamming his body against the bigger horse's torso.

"Pull him up and get him out of there," Mr. Griffen warned, as if Rhoda could hear him. "That two-year-old is going to knock Aladdin into the rail!"

Ashleigh felt her heart thud against her ribs. The horses were right below them now, and Ashleigh could see Aladdin's ears flick back and forth in confusion as the younger colt continued to bang against him with every stride.

Clever Patrol's jockey had the colt's head tipped as far to the right as he could, trying to get him to lay off Aladdin, but it wasn't working. Rhoda slowed Aladdin's pace, backing him a half length off Clever Patrol so his head was in the center of the two-year-old's body.

The next moment played before Ashleigh's eyes in slow motion as Clever Patrol cut across Aladdin's front legs in his effort to get to the inside rail. Rhoda pulled at the reins, trying to help Aladdin gain his balance.

"No!" Ashleigh screamed, and jumped from her chair. She watched in horror as Aladdin stumbled to his knees, sending Rhoda flying over his shoulder.

The blood pounded in Ashleigh's ears, drowning out the gasps of the people around her as they watched the terrible spectacle below.

Rhoda tumbled beneath the hooves of Clever Patrol, while Aladdin slid along the ground on his side, his legs scrambling to get a foothold on the track.

Ashleigh's heart seemed to stop altogether as Aladdin came to a halt against the post of the inside rail, lying still for a moment before he floundered around, his legs flailing in the air, and finally scrambled to his feet. He stood, momentarily stunned, then shook himself and took off at a gallop, heading for the track exit. Ashleigh saw movement along the outside rail and knew that Mike was racing toward the scene of the accident.

Aladdin seemed to be unhurt, and Ashleigh felt a faint flutter of relief. But when her eyes scanned the track, looking for Rhoda, she saw the jockey was lying faceup in the dirt, unmoving.

Ashleigh held her breath, expecting the usually energetic girl to get up and dust herself off. The heavy silence of the crowd was unsettling as everyone watched and waited. Still Rhoda didn't budge.

The next movement Ashleigh saw was the paramedics hopping the fence and sprinting toward the downed rider.

Was Rhoda all right? Was she dead? Ashleigh crushed her napkin in her hands. It felt as if she would never be able to breathe again.

4

Breakfast plates were forgotten as everyone looked on in shock. A low murmur rippled through the crowd as the paramedics knelt beside Rhoda, checking for injuries.

Ashleigh gripped the back of her chair, her knuckles turning white with the strain. *Rhoda has to be all right!* her mind screamed. *She was just galloping Aladdin a minute ago. How could she be lying so still in the dirt?* It just didn't seem possible.

A cold chill washed over Ashleigh. This was the fear she'd heard whispered about among riders, the reality of being a jockey: Horses were large, powerful animals, and sometimes their riders got badly hurt or even killed.

Ashleigh felt a comforting hand on her shoulder. She turned to meet her mother's worried gaze.

"The steward said she seems to be conscious," she said. "Mike is heading out onto the track. Since the outrider went after Aladdin, Mike probably wants to make sure his rider is all right before he goes back to the barn." Ashleigh stared at her mother. She had been so transfixed by the scene on the track that she hadn't noticed her mother get up to talk to one of the stewards.

"Can I go down there with Mike? I want to make sure Rhoda and Aladdin are okay."

Mrs. Griffen shook her head. "I don't think you should go down there right now. You don't want to get in the way of the medics."

Tears began to blur Ashleigh's vision. She felt helpless and trapped. *I can't do anything from up here.* She couldn't even tell if Rhoda was okay. And Aladdin needed her. She just knew it. She felt a tear slipping down her cheek, and she quickly brushed it away.

Mr. Griffen put an arm around Ashleigh's shoulders. "I'll go down with Ashleigh," he said to his wife. "We'll check on Rhoda, then go to the backside to see if there's anything we can do for Aladdin."

Mrs. Griffen brushed at another tear that was sliding down Ashleigh's cheek. "We'll get the car and meet you and your father at the stable." She placed a kiss on Ashleigh's forehead. "They'll be okay, Ash. They're both pretty tough."

Ashleigh nodded and forced a smile for her parents. She didn't think she could speak past the lump in her throat. She followed her father through the restaurant and out to the track. A security guard stopped them at first but then allowed them to pass when Mike waved them through.

"Is she going to be okay?" Ashleigh tried to see around the paramedics, but they hovered over the downed rider. Ashleigh swallowed the lump rising in her throat. She didn't know Rhoda all that well, but she felt a bond with the jockey. It was terrible to see her like that.

One of the medics moved, and Ashleigh caught a glimpse of Rhoda lying flat on her back in the dirt. Her helmet had been removed, and her hair was matted with dirt and sweat.

Ashleigh held her breath and stepped closer to the medics, wanting desperately to help. Rhoda must have felt the sunlight being blocked, because she turned her head and opened her eyes. When she saw Ashleigh, her pained expression was replaced by recognition and she smiled.

Ashleigh let out her breath and heaved a sigh of relief. Rhoda's smile told her all she needed to know— the dark-haired jockey was going to be all right.

Mike stood watch over Rhoda while the medics hurried to the ambulance for a stretcher. "You gave us a pretty good scare, Rhoda. How do you feel?"

Rhoda shrugged. "A little stiff. I want to get up, but the medics won't let me."

Ashleigh drew closer as the medical team hoisted Rhoda onto the stretcher. "I'm so glad you're okay." Her voice squeaked a little, but Ashleigh didn't care.

Rhoda flashed her a smile and gave a thumbs-up sign. "Don't let this scare you too much, Ashleigh. It's all part of being a jockey. Sometimes you take a few hard knocks." She winced as the paramedics lifted the stretcher and began to walk across the dirt track toward the ambulance. "It's still the best job in the world."

They watched as Rhoda was loaded into the ambulance. Mike turned to Mr. Griffen, who was running a nervous hand through his graying hair. "I wanted to make sure Rhoda was okay, but I've got to get back to Aladdin. I may need some help. Can you come with me?" Mike asked.

"Sure," Mr. Griffen said.

Ashleigh followed close behind as they jogged around the outside of the track toward the stables. Her lungs were burning by the time they reached the gate, but she didn't care. She had to make sure Aladdin was all right.

Mr. Griffen pulled off his jacket and draped it over his arm, rolling up his sleeves to prepare to help. "What were they doing, working that green two-year-old colt before he was ready to breeze? I thought they kept the wild ones on the small training track until they had some manners."

Mike shook his head in disgust. "I know they've been having trouble with that colt. I guess they thought they had him figured out."

One of the other trainers saw them hurrying off the track and stepped out of his shed row to flag them down. "Your horse ran into the machine yard, where they keep all the tractors and plows," he said.

"Oh, no." Ashleigh groaned, worry tying her stomach into a knot. The machine yard was where they took horses that had been hurt so badly they had to be destroyed. It had a high slatted fence, so you couldn't see into it. If a horse needed to be put to sleep, it was better to do it out of the public eye.

The track veterinarian's blue truck pulled up to the machine yard fence. Little patches of gray began to blur Ashleigh's vision, and her breath came in short gasps. She felt her father's hand reach out to steady her.

"Are you all right, Ash?" Mr. Griffen asked.

"They can't put him down!" She clutched at her father's hand. "Don't let them do this!"

Mike put an encouraging arm around Ashleigh's trembling shoulders. "We don't even know if he's hurt," he said. "Let's not assume the worst."

"But he's in the machine yard," Ashleigh protested. "And the vet's here."

"That's true, but we shouldn't jump to conclusions," Mike said. "After all, we saw Aladdin canter off the track."

They reached the gate at the same time as the track vet. "How is he?" Mike asked.

Dr. Elliott stroked his close-cropped beard. "I haven't looked at the colt yet. I just got the call that he was in with the tractors. I guess this is where he ran when he came off the track."

They stepped into the machine yard and stopped. At the very back corner of the enclosure, where the plows were parked so close together that there was hardly a foot between them, Aladdin stood with his head down and his reins dangling. His gallop saddle was turned onto his belly, and his foam-flecked sides still heaved from exertion and fear.

"Poor boy," Ashleigh said as she moved to go to the black colt.

"Just a second, miss," an old man in grease-soaked coveralls called out. "We're not sure how that colt got into that corner without tearing himself up on all those sharp plows, but I don't think he'll be as lucky the second time around." He pulled off his old, rumpled hat and wiped his brow. "If something spooks that colt and he tries to come back across those harrows, he won't be good for running anymore."

"But what can we do?" Ashleigh demanded of the

circle of men who stood around her. There wasn't time to ponder the situation. "How will we get him out of there?" Aladdin was surrounded by high fences on two sides, and the row of plows blocked him in the front. It looked like an impossible situation.

"I've got a tranquilizer for him," the vet said, and began stepping carefully through the tractor blades, but Aladdin snorted and lifted his head, prancing nervously in place as though he was preparing to bolt across the plows to get away from the veterinarian.

"Wait!" Mike hollered. "As scared as Aladdin is, I don't think he'll let you near him right now."

"We've got to do something!" Ashleigh said.

"Is he your horse?" the man in the coveralls asked.

Ashleigh shook her head. "No, but he was raised on my family's farm. I've spent a lot of time with him. He knows me."

The old man turned to Mike and Mr. Griffen. "We need someone to distract him while I move that tractor and plow. There's not very much room back there, but I'd say the girl might be small enough to get in there and calm the colt down." He slapped his hat back on his head and pulled it low over his eyes. "But if the colt blows up when I bring the tractor around, she might get hurt, too."

Ashleigh looked at Aladdin. His chest was scratched and bleeding, his head was down, and he was quivering from nose to tail. Ashleigh would do whatever she could to help him.

Mike turned to Ashleigh and her father. "It could be dangerous if the colt panics. How do you feel about this, Ashleigh?"

Ashleigh squared her shoulders. She knew Aladdin trusted her. She was the best hope the colt had of getting out of this mess. Even though she was scared to death, she knew she had to try.

"I don't know about this, Ash," Mr. Griffen said worriedly as he surveyed the small area that Ashleigh would have to work in. "It looks very dangerous."

Ashleigh gave him a nervous smile. "I know, Dad, but Aladdin needs me. I can do it."

Mr. Griffen ruffled her hair. "I get the feeling that even if I told you no, you'd figure out some way to do it anyway. Just promise me that at the first sign of trouble you'll get out of there."

Ashleigh nodded. "I will. But don't worry, it'll be okay." She walked up to the harrows, swallowing hard as she stared at the hundreds of twelve-inch iron spikes that made up the plowing surface of the harrow. The plows were parked less than a foot apart— enough room for her to pass through safely. But how had Aladdin made it through, and how would he get out?

Ashleigh kept her eyes on Aladdin and carefully

walked through the maze of sharp steel. Aladdin snorted and rolled his eyes as she approached, but Ashleigh spoke softly to him, trying to calm his fears.

"Easy, boy," Ashleigh crooned as she approached the colt. Aladdin's ears pricked at the sound of her voice, and he turned his head toward her. "That's a good boy," she encouraged him as she reached out to scoop up the broken reins.

Ashleigh placed a hand on Aladdin's neck, feeling his muscles tremble beneath her palm. "Good boy, Aladdin," she whispered, running her hand down his white blaze. "Easy."

"Keep a tight hold on those reins," Dr. Elliott instructed. "If he tries to bolt when they start the tractor, drop the reins and get out of the way. We don't want you getting hurt."

Ashleigh nodded and grabbed the reins under Aladdin's chin, giving them a gentle shake to distract the colt.

"Ready?" the old man said, and turned the ignition key on the tractor, preparing to pull it around to hook it up to the plow.

Aladdin snorted as the tractor roared to life. He tossed his head in the air, nearly jerking Ashleigh off the ground as he backed up and hit the fence behind him, dragging Ashleigh with him.

"Get out of there, Ash!" she heard her father yell, but Ashleigh knew that if she let go, Aladdin would charge through the plows and permanently damage himself.

The man killed the engine and jumped from the tractor. "Is she okay?"

"I'm all right," Ashleigh called, her voice shaking, as Aladdin lowered his head and she felt her heels touch the ground again. "Easy, big guy." Ashleigh scratched Aladdin along the cheekbones, trying to get his attention off the tractor, but her hands trembled so badly she could hardly control them.

"We're going to have to do this by hand," Mike said, stepping forward to the head of the plow. "I think there's enough of us that we can move the harrow a little at a time, so the colt doesn't spook."

"Good idea," Mr. Griffen said as he moved into position beside the trainer. "Are you all right, Ash?"

"Yes," Ashleigh croaked in reply. She stroked Aladdin's neck, over and over.

The men lined up along the sides of the harrow, bending and grabbing the edges of the plow with their hands. Smiles were traded all around as they moved the harrow the first several inches and Aladdin stayed quiet. Everyone worked quickly. Aladdin's head rose briefly when the plow grazed the one next to it and a sharp metallic scraping noise sounded, but Ashleigh jiggled the reins to distract him, and he quieted down once more.

When the harrow had been pulled forward and

moved off to the side, there was an eight-foot path to lead Aladdin through. "Let's go, boy," Ashleigh said as she pulled on the reins.

Aladdin took a step, but the dangling stirrups banged against his legs, and the colt halted abruptly, his eyes rolling in fear.

Ashleigh turned to her father and Mike. "I can't reach the saddle."

Mike stepped forward cautiously. "Maybe he'll let me hold him while you slip around and pull the buckles on the girth."

Ashleigh spoke encouragingly to Aladdin while Mike walked toward them. The colt snorted once but accepted Mike's hands on the reins. Ashleigh patted Aladdin on the shoulder and stepped to his side, quickly undoing the girth and catching the saddle before it fell to the ground.

There was a collective sigh of relief from the onlookers as Ashleigh handed the saddle to Mike and took the broken reins once more. She clucked softly to Aladdin, and the big horse took one tentative step forward, then another. His nostrils flared as he tilted his head, looking at the harrows on either side of the path, trying to catch their scent.

"It's okay, boy," Ashleigh assured him as they moved forward another couple of steps. "They're not going to move. You'll be okay."

Aladdin followed Ashleigh into the clearing, side-stepping when everyone clapped as they moved out of the danger zone.

Mike rushed forward to take Aladdin, and Mr. Griffen hugged Ashleigh to him. "You did it, Ashleigh!" he said proudly. "You saved him."

"But he might be hurt," Ashleigh said worriedly. "Look at those scrapes on his chest."

The vet stepped forward and opened his medical bag, taking out his stethoscope and listening to Aladdin's heart before he ran his hands over the colt's legs and body, checking for any unsoundness. "Can you jog him a few steps for me?" he asked Mike.

Ashleigh held her breath as the small crowd of trainers and grooms parted to give Aladdin room. Aladdin had to be all right. He just had to be sound. She watched as Mike clucked and jogged off. Aladdin tossed his head in the air and snorted at the sudden movement, but when he understood what was expected of him, he trotted beside the trainer.

"Looks good to me," the vet said when Aladdin and Mike stopped in front of him. "He's got a couple of deep scratches, but other than that, I'd say he's going to be fine. I'll give you some ointment to put on those scrapes." He turned to Ashleigh and smiled. "Thanks to this little lady, I'd say you'll still be running at Churchill Downs in two weeks."

Thank goodness Aladdin was all right! Ashleigh gave Aladdin one last pat, then followed her father up to the track cafeteria. Since Mike hadn't been able to give the okay for her mother, Caroline, and Rory to come onto the backside, it was likely that they were waiting for them there.

Ashleigh gave all of the details of Aladdin's rescue to the rest of the family on the drive home. Her mother had called the hospital while they were waiting and checked on Rhoda's condition. Rhoda was being kept for observation for a night, but she would be released the next day.

When they had finished discussing all the details, Ashleigh leaned her head against the car's window and closed her eyes. She kept seeing the crash again and again in her mind. The doctors had said that Aladdin and Rhoda would be fine, but how could they be, after an accident like that? It was something Ashleigh would remember for a long time. Could Rhoda and Aladdin just forget about it?

The car came to a stop in front of their farmhouse. Ashleigh opened her eyes and stepped out of the car. "I'm going to visit Stardust and get started on my stalls," she said.

"How about if you make a quick trip to the house to change into your barn clothes first?" her mother suggested sternly.

Ashleigh rolled her eyes but trotted off to the house. She didn't understand why her mother was so fussy. The horse smell would come out when the clothes were washed. What was the big deal?

She entered the house and headed up the stairs to change, then quickly ran down to the barn. If she could get through her stalls quickly, she would have time to spend with Stardust before dinner. She had a report due in English on Monday, and a quiz in math, but those could wait until after she ate. Right then she needed the comfort she got from spending time with her horse.

Ashleigh gathered the wheelbarrow and pitchfork and started on the first of her stalls. Caroline and Rory soon joined her. Caroline took the stall across from Ashleigh so they could talk about the day's events, and Rory busied himself with filling water buckets and collecting empty hay nets.

Jonas had the night off, so Ashleigh's parents mixed all the feed and hung the hay nets, then brought the mares and foals into the barn.

"I'll be up in a few minutes," Ashleigh said as the rest of her family went to the house to get dinner ready. Ashleigh grabbed a lead rope and went to fetch Stardust from the pasture. Just being next to the chestnut mare made her feel better.

Ashleigh hooked Stardust in the crossties and

picked up a brush, flicking the dirt out of the mare's copper coat with swift, even strokes. The simple routine calmed her down, but she couldn't keep bothersome thoughts from drifting through her mind.

She had heard of horses that had been in bad accidents and could never get up the will to run again. What if that happened to Aladdin?

Ashleigh finished Stardust's grooming, then spent a couple of minutes playing a new game with her. Ashleigh broke a carrot in pieces and hid one of the sections in her hand. She held both her closed fists up for Stardust's inspection, letting the mare nuzzle the hand she wanted.

Ashleigh laughed when the mare guessed right every time. "You've got a nose like a hunting dog's," she said as she put the mare in her stall and removed her halter. She put the halter in the tack room, then returned to the house.

Ashleigh pushed open the door. The house was filled with the smell of lasagna. Her mother always kept a couple of frozen casseroles and pasta dishes for nights when they were running late and didn't have time to cook.

Ashleigh pulled off her boots, then padded to the kitchen in her socks. The house was awfully quiet. She stepped into the kitchen and was greeted by a shushing noise from her mother.

"Dad's talking to Mike," Caroline whispered as Ashleigh took a seat beside her at the kitchen table.

Anxiously Ashleigh listened to bits of her father's conversation, hoping to piece together what was being said. After a minute her father hung up.

"What is it?" Ashleigh asked, worried that there was bad news about Rhoda or Aladdin.

Mr. Griffen took his seat at the head of the table. "Mike says Aladdin won't settle down. He keeps pacing his stall and digging. He spoke to Mr. Danworth tonight, and they want to move Aladdin someplace where he can get some peace and quiet before the Derby." He smiled at their expectant faces. "Aladdin's coming back to Edgardale."

5

Ashleigh sat on the couch with her legs drawn under her. Prince Charming, her Maine coon kitten, purred loudly from her lap. She held the telephone receiver in one hand and petted the kitten with the other.

"Aladdin is coming back to Edgardale?" Mona's excited voice came across the phone line.

Ashleigh switched the phone to her other ear and scratched Prince Charming under the chin. "I wish it were all good news," Ashleigh said. "But Aladdin's coming to Edgardale because of the accident he had at the track today."

Ashleigh explained what had happened at Breakfast with the Works. "Mike is going to talk to Rhoda tomorrow. Since she's signed a contract with the Danworths to be Aladdin's jockey for the Derby, she'll need to be close so she can gallop him. My parents have offered to let her stay here." Ashleigh felt a smile tugging at the corners of her mouth. She hoped Rhoda would accept the offer.

Mike had arranged to work Aladdin at the Wortons' training track next door when he recovered from the accident. Since the Wortons' farm was so close, it only made sense that Rhoda would want to stay at Edgardale.

"Just one more thing, Ash, before we hang up," Mona said. "The outline for our speech is due Tuesday. Have you decided what subject you're doing for your oral report?"

Ashleigh leaned against the cushions, lifting her feet so that one of Rory's play trucks wouldn't run over her toes. With all the excitement over Aladdin, she had forgotten about the report. "I'm not sure."

Ashleigh felt a familiar fluttering in her stomach. She always got the jitters when she thought about speaking in front of an audience. She didn't think she would be able to do it; it was just too scary. Maybe she could pretend to be sick and stay home that day.

But if I don't give the speech, I'll fail the project. Ashleigh sighed. She had a strong B in English, and she didn't want to blow it. Her eyes wandered around the room and landed on a book her father had left sitting on top of the end table. On the cover was a photo of an old sailing ship.

"Ships," Ashleigh told Mona. "I'm going to do my report on ships."

There was a long pause before Mona spoke again. "Ships? You mean, like, big boats? I don't know, Ash . . . what do you know about boats?"

Ashleigh picked the book off the table and opened it, running her eyes over the beautiful pictures of sailing ships. There was enough information in the book to cover a five-minute report.

"Yes, sailing ships." Ashleigh smiled, as if to congratulate herself. "Anyway, I have to go now, Mona. I'll see you at school tomorrow." She hung up and tucked the book under her arm. She could write the report easily. But giving it in front of the class was another thing.

Aladdin was delivered to Edgardale on Monday morning. They turned him loose in a large stall with a big connecting paddock, and he seemed to be content. There still wasn't any word on Rhoda's decision, but when Ashleigh got home from school on Tuesday afternoon, there was a little red car parked in front of the house.

Ashleigh ran all the way to the house, letting the screen door bang shut behind her as she rushed to find her mother.

"Hi, Ashleigh," Rory said from the kitchen table as he took a homemade chocolate chip cookie from the plate their mother held out.

Ashleigh giggled at the sight that greeted her.

"What's so funny?" Mrs. Griffen said.

Ashleigh pointed to her mother's stall-mucking boots and white cooking apron. "Those don't go very well together." She laughed.

Mrs. Griffen laughed, too. "When our guest showed up, I was mucking stalls with your father and Jonas. I wanted to hurry and get these baked so you'd have a treat to share with your new roommate."

Ashleigh set her book bag on the counter and took the cookies and sodas her mother handed her. "Rhoda's here?" she asked excitedly. "She's staying in our room?"

Mrs. Griffen nodded. "That was Rhoda's idea. She knew you two would have a lot to talk about. She's upstairs unpacking now," her mother said as she untied the apron and hung it over the towel rack. "Caro is going to sleep in Rory's bed, and Rory will sleep on the cot in our room."

Ashleigh was thrilled at the prospect of sharing a room with her idol. But her smile slipped from her face when she remembered how dirty her side of the room had been when she left for school this morning. She swallowed hard. Rhoda was going to think she was a slob.

Ashleigh took the snacks and headed for the staircase. She paused at the bottom of the stairs when she heard her mother calling to her. "Yes, Mom?"

Mrs. Griffen poked her head around the corner. "Don't grill Rhoda with a hundred questions, okay? She's going to be here until the Derby. You'll have plenty of time to talk. And I think she needs to get some rest—she's still a little shaken from the accident."

Ashleigh nodded and marched quickly up the stairs. She stopped outside her room. She was surprised at how nervous she felt. She hadn't been this jittery when she met movie star Kevin Donnelly, star of the horse television series *Old Red and Me,* at the Danworths' house. She pressed her shoulder against the door and gave it a shove. "Hi," she said to the dark-haired girl, who was taking clothes out of her suitcase.

"Hi there," Rhoda said as she transferred the contents of her bag to the dresser next to the bed. "I really want to thank you and your sister for letting me stay in this room. I told your parents I'd be okay out in the barn, but they wouldn't hear of it."

"Oh, n-no, you couldn't stay there," Ashleigh stammered. "You're too important!" She felt the color rising in her cheeks. Why did she always say something silly when she was around Rhoda?

Rhoda laughed. "Not really," she said. She held up a pair of socks with holes in the heels and shook her head. "Look at these. I'm just a normal person who loves to ride horses so much, I do it for a living."

"Someday I'm going to ride for a living, too," Ashleigh said. She sat down on the end of Caroline's bed and held out the soda and cookies. "I brought you a snack."

"Great." Rhoda smiled as she reached for a handful of cookies. "Some jockeys have to diet all the time, but luckily for me, I don't ever have to watch what I eat. Anytime you want to do a midnight raid on the refrigerator, you just let me know."

Ashleigh laughed, then stuffed a cookie into her mouth. Having Rhoda around was going to be a lot of fun. "Do you still hurt from the fall you took the other day?" Ashleigh asked.

Rhoda stretched her arms and legs out, as if searching for sore spots. "I have a few bruises, but I was very lucky that crazy colt didn't step all over me when I rolled under his hooves."

Ashleigh nodded. "We were really worried when you were just lying there."

Rhoda shrugged. "It's a dangerous job. But you have to try to forget about the bad times. And when you win, there's nothing like it."

Ashleigh gathered up her soda can and the cookie plate. Then she had an idea. "I've got to go clean my stalls before dinner. If you're not too tired, would you like to go for a ride and see the farm later? You could ride my mare, Stardust. She's really nice."

"That would be great," Rhoda agreed. She drank the rest of the soda and wiped the cookie crumbs from her chin. "I'd really like to see Edgardale, and I'm anxious to get back on a horse again and see if I can ride without aching too much." She laughed. "I think I'll lie down and rest a little before dinner. I'll see you later."

Ashleigh quickly changed into jeans and headed for the stable. She stopped by the front paddock on the way to the barn and called for Stardust. "How're you doing, girl?" she said as she rubbed the mare's neck and ran her fingers through her mane. "Isn't it good to have Aladdin back again?"

Ashleigh startled Jonas by coming into the barn from the paddock door.

"You think you're one of the horses now?" he joked as he ran a hand across the gray stubble on his chin. "Rory heard you were home. He's getting Moe tacked up. I think he's hoping you'll watch him ride."

Ashleigh went to Moe's stall and peeked in at her little brother and the pony. "Make sure you smooth his hair down under that pad before you put your saddle on," she reminded him.

"Are you going to watch me ride, Ashleigh?" Rory asked hopefully.

They had only an hour before dinner, and Ashleigh

had to finish her stalls, but Rory wouldn't get to ride unless someone was watching him. She didn't want to take Rory on her ride with Rhoda. She'd need to borrow the pony for herself.

"I'll make you a deal, Rory." Ashleigh stepped into the stall and helped her brother put the bridle over Moe's fuzzy ears. "I'll watch you ride if you let me borrow Moe after dinner."

Rory's head snapped up. "But you've got Stardust. Moe's mine now. You don't need to ride him."

"Rhoda wants to see the farm," Ashleigh said. "So I'm loaning her Stardust. There's no other horse here I can ride."

She could see the stubborn set to Rory's jaw. "I'll do your stalls today," she added. That seemed to change Rory's mind.

"Okay, but first you have to watch me ride for a *long* time," Rory said as he plopped his riding helmet down on his head and buckled the chin strap.

Ashleigh opened the stall door to let them out. "It's a deal. You'll have to ride in one of the paddocks near the manure pile, though, so I can watch you and get my stalls done at the same time. And no galloping if I'm not right there by the fence," she warned.

Rory smiled as he mounted the fuzzy little pony and headed for the paddock.

Ashleigh loaded up her wheelbarrow with dirty bedding, keeping an eye on Rory as she worked. Soon she'd be riding the trails with Rhoda! She was so happy, she even cleaned Caroline's stalls. When she was finished, she watched Rory canter a figure eight, then she helped him untack Moe. Rory was all smiles as they walked back to the house and washed up for supper.

Rhoda was bombarded with questions over dinner and hardly had a chance to eat. Ashleigh was impressed with Rhoda's tales of races won and lost. She couldn't wait till the day she'd have jockey stories of her own to tell.

When Caroline got started on the dishes, Ashleigh rushed out to the barn to ready the horses while Rhoda changed clothes. She had just snapped Stardust into the crossties when Rhoda walked in. The jockey stopped next to the chestnut mare and ran a hand over her sleek red coat.

"What a pretty mare. Is this Stardust?"

Ashleigh nodded. "You can ride her. I'm going to ride Rory's pony, Moe."

Aladdin poked his head over the stall door halfway down the barn and nickered.

"How's the big guy settling in?" Rhoda asked, and started to walk toward Aladdin's stall.

Ashleigh followed Rhoda. She was surprised when Aladdin snorted and backed up into the corner of his stall. "What's the matter, boy?" Ashleigh held her hand out to entice him back to the door, but Aladdin stayed where he was, looking warily at Rhoda.

"That's odd," Rhoda said. "Aladdin always has his head over the door at the track. Something must have spooked him."

"Maybe he's just a little jumpy today," Ashleigh replied. She gave up trying to lure the black colt toward her and turned to get Moe from his paddock. Quickly she and Rhoda tacked up the two horses and led them out into the stable yard.

Rhoda checked her equipment and mounted up, wincing as she settled into the saddle. "I guess I'm still a little sore," she said with a laugh.

Ashleigh led the way out of the barn and turned Moe onto the nearest trail. Rhoda did look uncomfortable, but Ashleigh hoped the soreness would wear off soon, because Aladdin was going to need exercise. There were only eleven days left until the Derby.

"I heard some trainers say bad things about Aladdin," Ashleigh said. "They think he won the Blue Grass by accident. Is that true? Would Star Gazer have beaten Aladdin if he hadn't acted up?"

Rhoda followed Ashleigh down the trail. "No way. Aladdin had even more to give coming off that last turn. I think they would have had a tough time beating him." She smiled at Ashleigh. "Anyway, we've only got a week and a half until we'll know for sure."

Ashleigh showed Rhoda some of her favorite trails, then led the way back to the barn. "I want to show you all our broodmares. Aladdin's mother is here, too," Ashleigh said with pride. "Her name is Go Gen."

Jonas was giving the barn aisle its final sweep when the girls rode into the stable area.

"This is Jonas," Ashleigh said, introducing Rhoda to the groom as she pulled the saddles off Stardust and Moe and put them in the tack room.

"You must be Rhoda," he said with a smile, and shook her hand. "Ashleigh talks about you all the time." Jonas picked up a brush and started on the mare and pony. "I'll finish these up for you, Ashleigh, so you can spend some more time with your idol."

Ashleigh quickly led Rhoda away before Jonas could mention that a few weeks earlier she'd put a saddle on a sawhorse in the tack room and pretended to be Rhoda riding Aladdin in the Derby. That would be way too embarrassing!

"What a great place to grow up," Rhoda said as she followed Ashleigh out to the broodmare paddocks. "You're really lucky, Ashleigh."

They stepped through the fence into the paddock. "Here, girls," Ashleigh called. She pulled a few carrots out of her pocket and broke them into pieces. The closest broodmares lifted their heads at the sound of snapping carrots and meandered forward, their new foals following close behind.

"This is Althea and her new colt, and Marvy Mary and her filly," Ashleigh said as she offered a carrot to each of the mares. "Go Gen is the gray. She's Aladdin's dam, and that's her new black filly. Her name is Shadow—she's a full sister to Aladdin."

Shadow walked right up to them, her little broom of a tail swishing as she poked her muzzle at Rhoda and Ashleigh. Ashleigh giggled, fending off the black filly's nuzzling lips. New foals got their front teeth within a few days of being born, and they liked to nip. Their playmates might not mind, but Ashleigh knew from experience that it could really hurt.

Mr. Griffen came around the corner of the barn with an armful of halters and lead ropes. "There you are," he said as he caught Go Gen and Althea. "Your mother and I were looking for you two. We should have known you'd both be out with the horses."

Ashleigh and Rhoda took some of the halters and helped him catch the mares so that they could lead them into the barn for the night.

"Mike called," Mr. Griffen said, glancing at Rhoda as he put the mare and foal he was leading into their stall.

"Oh?" Rhoda said, handing him Marvy Mary's lead.

"Mike wants to give Aladdin a good gallop at the Wortons' track on Thursday," Mr. Griffen said. "But he thinks it might go better if you take him out on the trails so he can relax. I suggested you go out with Ashleigh tomorrow after she gets home from school."

"All right!" Ashleigh said. She was beginning to worry that Aladdin was going to lose some of his conditioning if they didn't get him out of that stall soon. It was one thing to rest a horse, but you couldn't win the Kentucky Derby on stall rest.

But the look on Rhoda's face wasn't what Ashleigh had expected. She looked hesitant and scared—anything but excited. *Oh, no,* Ashleigh thought. With only eleven days left until the Derby, it looked as though they were heading for more trouble.

6

That night as the rest of the household slept, Ashleigh turned on her side to face Rhoda's bed. "You awake?" she whispered.

"You can't sleep, either?" Rhoda said groggily as she propped herself up on one elbow.

Ashleigh stared into the blackness of the bedroom. She wasn't sure if she should ask or not, but she just had to know. "Rhoda, are you nervous about riding Aladdin tomorrow?"

The silence in the room stretched out for so long that Ashleigh thought Rhoda had drifted off to sleep. She was just about to close her own eyes when the answer came.

"Maybe a little."

Ashleigh leaned back against her pillow, staring blindly up at the ceiling. "I got bucked off Stardust when I first got her, and I didn't want to get back on," she admitted. "My dad made me. He said that if I didn't get right back on, I'd lose my confidence and Stardust might decide that bucking was okay."

Ashleigh paused, unsure if she should continue. Who was she to be giving advice to a great jockey? But Aladdin's and Rhoda's careers were at stake. What did she have to lose? "Sometimes it's really hard, and it's really scary, but if you don't get back on your horse, you'll never be able to ride with the same confidence again."

Ashleigh waited, wondering if Rhoda was going to laugh or get mad at her.

Rhoda pulled the covers up to her chin and sighed. "You're right," she said into the dark room. She turned over to face the wall. "Good night, Ash. I'll see you when you get home from school tomorrow."

Ashleigh smiled as she drifted off to sleep. Everything would work out. It just had to!

"I can't believe you got an A on your oral report outline," Mona said as they stepped off the school bus on Wednesday afternoon.

Ashleigh hefted her book bag over her shoulder. "Why not? I always get good grades in English."

Mona stared at her paper, which was covered with red pen marks. "I know, but you only spent an hour working on it. I spent two days on mine, and I only got a B minus."

Ashleigh stopped at the head of her driveway and frowned. "Yeah, but when you have to stand up in front of the class and give your report, you'll get an A, and I'll probably faint and get an F."

Mona stuffed her paper into her backpack. "Is it really that bad, Ash? Does it scare you that much?"

Ashleigh nodded her head. "Just thinking about it gives me a stomachache."

Mona smiled in sympathy. "You'd better think of something quick. We've got to give these reports next Monday."

Ashleigh laughed. "I've already thought of something. It's called staying home with the flu." She waved to Mona as she headed to her own house. "I'm going riding with Rhoda this afternoon. Do you want me to ask if you can come?"

"Sure," Mona said. "Frisky would love to meet Aladdin, especially now that he's a Kentucky Derby horse. I've got to clean my stalls first. I'll meet you at your barn in an hour."

Ashleigh laughed. "Just remember . . . no racing!"

Ashleigh cut through the paddocks to say hello to Stardust and Aladdin, then entered the barn. Her mother was forking dirty bedding into a wheelbarrow.

"You'd better hurry and get changed for your trail

ride," Mrs. Griffen said when she saw her. "Rhoda is up at the house with Mike."

Ashleigh grabbed the full wheelbarrow, pushing it out to the manure pile. "Do you think it would be all right if Mona comes with us?" she called over her shoulder.

Mr. Griffen poked his head out of the end stall, where he had been hanging a hay net. "That's up to the trainer. You'd better ask him. He might not want a lot of horses around Aladdin—we don't want him getting all worked up. They brought Aladdin to Edgardale to settle him down, remember."

Ashleigh parked the wheelbarrow in front of the stall. "Okay. I'd better go change my clothes so I can get my stalls finished before we go."

Mrs. Griffen stepped out of the stall and brushed a strand of blond hair off her damp forehead. "I'll do your stalls today, Ash. It's a beautiful day—you go ahead and enjoy your ride with Rhoda."

"Thanks, Mom. You're the best!"

Ashleigh ran to the house. Mike was sitting in a chair on the front porch, reading a racing magazine and sipping a glass of iced tea.

"Hey there. Are you ready for your trail ride with Aladdin?"

Ashleigh nodded vigorously. "Would it be okay if my friend Mona came along with us?" she asked.

"I don't see why not," Mike said. "Aladdin hasn't

been on a trail ride for a while. It might help if one of you girls rode ahead of him and one behind, so he doesn't get any ideas about running away."

"Great!" Ashleigh said. "I'll call Mona and tell her." She opened the front door and hurried up the stairs. When she entered her bedroom, Rhoda and Caroline were sitting on the bed looking through fashion magazines. Ashleigh was a little surprised that the jockey would be interested in dresses and shoes.

"Can you believe it?" Caroline said. "Rhoda has the same taste in clothes as I do. She's helping me pick a dress for the Derby."

Ashleigh threw her book bag on the bed. "Where do you want to go riding today?"

Rhoda shrugged her shoulders. "Those trails we took the other day were nice, but maybe we could find someplace with a big field. I'd like to teach you how to pony, so you'll be able to help with Aladdin. We can't have him running away with me on the way to the Wortons' track, can we?"

"Pony? Me?" Ashleigh forgave Rhoda for being interested in Caroline's fashion magazines. "That would be great!" she said, then hesitated. "But do you think I can? I've never ponied a racehorse before, and neither has Stardust."

Ashleigh thought about the time she had ridden Aladdin on the beach and he had run away with her.

What if she wasn't strong enough to pony him and Aladdin got away from her?

Rhoda smiled at Ashleigh. "Your mare handles very nicely, and the colt is easy to pony. Anyway, I'll be riding him, so I'll be able to guide him and make it easier."

Ashleigh pulled her homework out of her book bag. "I have to do my math homework and practice for a stupid oral report, but it will only take about a half hour. I'll meet you out at the barn." She headed for the staircase, stopping on the first step. "Rhoda?" she called. "I invited my friend Mona to go riding with us today. Is it okay if she comes?"

"Sure," Rhoda replied. "I'll meet you two in the barn in forty-five minutes."

Ashleigh ran down the stairs to call Mona and let her know that their ride was still on.

Ashleigh smiled at Mona over the top of Stardust's back as she dropped her mare's saddle pad into place. "This is going to be so cool!" She positioned her saddle and reached under the mare's belly to grab the girth.

Her mother and father were saddling Aladdin in the next set of crossties. The colt stomped his feet and tossed his head. The scrapes on his chest were healing nicely, and he looked fresh and ready to go. Rhoda leaned against the wall, frowning as she watched the black colt chomp at the bit.

Mr. Griffen pulled the girth up a notch, then unsnapped the crossties. "He's all yours." He gestured to Rhoda. "I'll give you a leg up outside."

Rhoda reached for the reins, but Aladdin snorted and jerked his head away.

"Whoa." Mr. Griffen reached out and stopped the colt, then waited for Rhoda to take the reins again.

Rhoda led the colt out of the barn. "Maybe I should longe him before we go for a ride."

Ashleigh thought she detected a note of concern in the jockey's voice. Was she worried that Aladdin would run off with her?

"I think he'll be okay," Mrs. Griffen said. "He's just restless to get on his way."

Rhoda accepted his leg up, then double-checked her girth. "Ashleigh, you lead the way, and Mona, you go behind us," Rhoda instructed. "I want Aladdin sandwiched in between your horses so he can't go anywhere."

Ashleigh nodded and asked her mare for a walk. Stardust moved down the familiar trail, her ears flicking back and forth, catching the sounds the big black colt made as he pranced behind her.

"Why won't he settle down?" Ashleigh heard Mona ask.

"He hasn't been ridden since last weekend," Rhoda answered, her voice tight with nerves.

Ashleigh looked over her shoulder. "We usually trot along this stretch. Are you ready?" she asked Rhoda.

The jockey shook her head. "Let's walk for a little while. Aladdin is used to being on the racetrack with rails to fence him in. I want to make sure he isn't going to take off when he sees all this open space."

Ashleigh frowned. Why was Rhoda so worried? Aladdin was really well behaved for a racehorse.

When they hit the trail that bordered a long fence, Rhoda agreed to trot. She clucked to Aladdin, but instead of breaking into the expected smooth trot, the colt suddenly bolted forward, bumping into Stardust.

Ashleigh patted the surprised mare's neck, speaking softly until Stardust settled down. "What was that?" she asked Rhoda after she got Stardust under control.

"Sorry," Rhoda said. "Aladdin is really feeling his oats today. We'd better pick up the trot and wear him down a bit before we teach you how to pony."

They bumped the horses back into a trot, and this time Aladdin went along smoothly. They trotted along an uphill path that led into the forest and out onto the field where Jessica's Jump was. Along the way, Rhoda asked Ashleigh and Mona about their schoolwork. Ashleigh told the jockey about her oral report and her fear of speaking in front of an audience.

"You know, I do some speaking at schools, luncheons, and horse clubs," Rhoda said. "I give talks on what it's like to be a jockey, and a female athlete in a male-dominated sport. Maybe I could help you."

"That would be great," Ashleigh said. "After the kids laughed at me that one time, I get so scared now that when I open my mouth nothing comes out, or I mix my words up and say the wrong thing."

Rhoda smiled. "That sounds like a classic case of stage fright. You've got to learn to control your fear." Just then they entered the pasture. "This is perfect," she said. "We can start here and gallop all the way across it."

"No!" Mona and Ashleigh cried in unison.

At Rhoda's questioning look, Ashleigh explained. "There's a really deep creek that runs through the middle of it. Let me show you." She asked Stardust for a slow trot, stopping several feet from the creek. They let their horses put their heads down to munch on the sweet, tall grass. Aladdin seemed to settle down, happy to follow along with the mares.

"Wow! I'm glad you said something." Rhoda stood in her stirrups to get a better view of the creek. "How far down is it?"

Ashleigh shivered. "Ten feet across and five feet down," she told Rhoda. "They call it Jessica's Jump because of a girl who took a dare and tried to jump it."

"You're kidding." Rhoda gave Ashleigh a skeptical look. "Nobody in their right mind would try that."

Ashleigh shook her head in sympathy. "The horse had to be put down, and Jessica went to the hospital. Maybe I should try the jump. That would be one way to get out of giving my oral report," she joked.

Rhoda pulled Aladdin's head up and turned to Ashleigh, her face deadly serious. "Don't even joke about that. It's easy enough to get hurt on a horse without purposely trying to. Promise me you'll never do something that crazy."

Mona giggled. "She almost tried it a few days ago, didn't you, Ash?"

Rhoda stared at Ashleigh.

"Not on purpose," Ashleigh said, defending herself. "I was upset about what happened in English. I just wanted to gallop, and I forgot the creek was here. But I pulled up at the last minute."

Rhoda shook her head and sighed. "You were very lucky. That would have been a horrible fall."

"Don't worry, I learned my lesson," Ashleigh said.

"How about we learn another lesson?" Rhoda pulled Aladdin's head up and walked him to Stardust's side, handing Ashleigh a long leather strap. "Run this through the ring on Aladdin's bit and double it back so you have equal lengths of strap."

Just then Aladdin took a nip at Stardust, and the mare sidestepped away.

"Knock it off, you big bruiser," Rhoda said as she tapped him with the end of the reins. "Just remember that racehorses are spirited. Some of them will try to nip at you or the pony horse. You need to keep his head right at the front of your saddle by your horse's shoulder."

"Like this?" Ashleigh said as she moved Aladdin into position and asked Stardust for a walk.

"That's it," Rhoda said. "Keep your arm bent at the elbow, but stiff, so he can't press against you. If he gets too far ahead or behind, you won't be able to control his head anymore and you can have some big problems." She looked over her shoulder at Mona. "Can you hear me, Mona? You can have a turn, too, if you like. You might as well both learn to do this if you're going to be around racehorses."

Ashleigh smiled nervously as they walked around the field. Aladdin tried nipping Stardust again, but Ashleigh caught him in time, keeping her arm stiff so that he couldn't reach her mare.

"That's it," Rhoda said encouragingly. "Let's ask them for a trot now and see if you can hold that position."

Aladdin took off at a faster pace than Stardust, but he slowed down when he felt the pressure from Ashleigh's lead strap, and matched his pace to the mare's.

"You're doing fine, Ash," Rhoda said as she posted in time to Aladdin's trot. "How's it feel?"

"Great!" Ashleigh grinned. "But my arm is really tired. It feels like it's ready to fall off!"

Rhoda pulled Aladdin back to a walk. "Okay, let's give Mona a turn, then we'll head home. The horses will get cranky if their dinner is late."

Rhoda spent another fifteen minutes working with Mona. Frisky was just as tall as Aladdin, so it was easier for Mona to control his head. But Aladdin kept his ears pinned—he seemed to like Stardust better.

"Can I pony you all the way back?" Ashleigh asked.

Rhoda relaxed her grip on the reins. "Sure. Aladdin goes much better with a pony horse, anyway."

As the horses trotted along, Ashleigh concentrated on keeping Aladdin in the right place. Her arm got sore in a hurry, and by the time they reached the barn, her muscles felt like mush.

"That was fun," Mona said as she turned Frisky down the driveway toward her house. "When does Aladdin start working out at the Wortons'?"

"Tomorrow," Rhoda said as she took the lead strap from Ashleigh and pulled Aladdin to a stop in front of the barn door. "You can come and watch anytime."

"That'd be great!" Mona waved and trotted Frisky down the driveway.

Mike and Jonas met them at the barn. "How'd it

go?" Mike asked as Ashleigh dismounted. "I'm going to be really sore tomorrow."

"I think it went pretty well." Rhoda grinned as she moved her leg forward and reached down to loosen the girth. "I was glad to have two pony horses with me, though. Aladdin was feeling pretty full of himself."

Aladdin flicked his ears at the rustle of clothing and the shifting of Rhoda's weight. He snorted and jumped to the side, throwing her off balance. Caught off guard, the young jockey threw her arms around Aladdin's neck and tried to push herself upright, but the colt spooked and bolted to the side. Rhoda crashed to the ground.

Rhoda jumped quickly to her feet and ran to grab Aladdin's reins, but the horse cut to the side and took off.

Rhoda stood with her hands on her hips, staring after Aladdin as Jonas and Mike ran to catch him. "What was that?" she said in dismay as she brushed the dirt from her clothing. "He was doing so well. Come on, Ash, we've got to catch him!"

Ashleigh jogged Stardust into her stall and ran after the others, praying that Aladdin wouldn't run down the driveway and get out onto the road. They were only ten days away from the Kentucky Derby. He couldn't hurt himself now.

7

Aladdin missed the turn up the driveway, galloping a lap around the barn and house with his tail cocked over his back and his nostrils flared. Ashleigh caught up to him by the broodmare paddock, where the stallion was sniffing noses with his dam and his little sister, Shadow.

"What do you think you're doing?" Ashleigh scolded the big colt. Aladdin stared at her and snorted nonchalantly. She snatched up his reins and patted his neck, glad to see he was in one piece.

"Is he all right?" Rhoda asked anxiously as she came around the barn.

Ashleigh nodded. "He's a little sweaty, but we were going to give him a bath anyway."

Mike came running across the lawn. "Thank goodness you caught him," he panted. He knelt down to check Aladdin's legs.

"Where's Jonas?" Ashleigh asked as she looked around the property.

Mike laughed. "We're old, Ashleigh. We can't keep up with you youngsters. I sent Jonas back to the barn to take care of your mare." He took Aladdin's lead rope from Ashleigh. "Let's get this big fella washed up and put back in his stall before he causes any more trouble."

They finished with Aladdin and said good-bye to Mike, then Ashleigh and Rhoda went up to the house to clean up for dinner.

"I'm sorry you fell off today," Ashleigh said to Rhoda as they walked up the steps to the house.

"Yeah, I seem to be doing a lot of that lately," Rhoda said as she sat down on a step and pulled off her boots, shaking out the dirt that had accumulated during their chase with Aladdin.

Ashleigh frowned. She knew Rhoda was trying to make a joke, but she could hear the worry in the jockey's voice. Ashleigh could tell that this latest fall had affected Rhoda more than she wanted to admit. "I'll see you inside," Rhoda said as she pushed through the door.

Ten minutes later everyone was seated at the dinner table. Ashleigh's stomach growled as she waited for the big plate of spaghetti to be passed her way.

She let Rory and Caroline do most of the talking while she stuffed herself with spaghetti. She hadn't had any idea how much strain ponying put on your arms or how hungry it could make you.

Rory was happy to be the center of attention. He talked nonstop about Moe and his riding lessons. Caroline was describing some new outfit she'd seen in a magazine that would be perfect to wear at the Kentucky Derby.

"Mr. Worton called tonight," Ashleigh's mother said when the meal was almost over. "They're all ready for Aladdin to begin his workouts there tomorrow."

Ashleigh glanced up from her last bite of spaghetti and nodded. "I learned how to pony on Stardust today. I'll be ponying Rhoda and Aladdin over to the Wortons' tomorrow."

Ashleigh noticed the way Rhoda lowered her eyes when Aladdin's name was mentioned. She hoped Rhoda wasn't losing faith in Aladdin or her ability to ride him. But after two falls she could see why Rhoda's confidence was shaken.

"We also got some disturbing news from the Wortons today," Mr. Griffen added.

All eyes turned to the head of the table.

Mr. Griffen wiped some sauce from his chin and continued. "Star Gazer is training at their track, too."

Rhoda paused with her fork halfway to her mouth.

"How did that happen? I thought Star Gazer was going to Churchill Downs to train." A frown settled heavily between her brows.

Ashleigh wasn't sure she liked the idea, either. Star Gazer was trouble. He was known for being a bully, and it was his little brother who had caused Aladdin's accident at Breakfast with the Works. She glanced at Rhoda, wondering if the jockey was thinking the same thing. "How could the Wortons let Star Gazer train at their farm?" Ashleigh demanded. "Why would they want him around?"

"What does Mike say about this?" Rhoda added.

Mrs. Griffen stood up to take her empty plate to the sink. "Mike hasn't made it back to his hotel room yet," she explained. "We'll try him again in a while. According to the Wortons, Star Gazer's trainer wanted to keep him out of the public eye for a while, and the owners are friends of the Wortons. That's why he's there."

"It was nice of them to warn us that Star Gazer is going to be there," Mr. Griffen said. "But the fact is, it's their farm and they can do anything they like with it. It's quite a boost for them to be able to say they have two Kentucky Derby horses training at their place."

Mr. Griffen rose and handed his dishes to his wife, helping clear the rest of the dirty plates from the table. "It shouldn't be a problem as long as we make sure the horses are being worked at different times. If it bothers Mike, we can always trailer Aladdin over to Shady Valley to train, like we did last time, but the less trailering you do, the less chance there is of a horse getting hurt on the road."

Rhoda cleared her throat and abruptly changed the subject. "Would you like to work on your speech after dinner, Ash?"

Ashleigh lifted her milk glass and grinned. "Not really," she joked. "But I know you won't let me say no." What Ashleigh really wanted to do was talk about Aladdin and how they were going to train at the Wortons' without running into Star Gazer, but Rhoda didn't seem to want to discuss it.

Ashleigh helped clear the rest of the table and wash the dishes. Something didn't feel right. Rhoda was bothered about something. Ashleigh hoped the next day's workout would go well. Then maybe Rhoda would feel better about riding Aladdin.

"Ready?" Rhoda asked when Ashleigh had finished the dishes.

Ashleigh nodded and followed her upstairs to the bedroom. Rhoda plopped herself down on the bed while Ashleigh found her report.

"Okay," Rhoda said, folding her hands behind her head and waiting expectantly.

Ashleigh shuffled the papers and stared at her. "Okay what?"

"Let's hear it." Rhoda smiled encouragingly.

Ashleigh rearranged the papers again, paused for a moment, then opened her mouth to speak. She closed it immediately and shifted her weight to her other foot, sneaking a peek at Rhoda.

Rhoda raised her brows. "Yes?"

Ashleigh swallowed hard. *It shouldn't be this hard to speak in front of just one person,* she thought. She took a deep breath and started again. "'Ships of the Eighteen Hundreds,' by Ashleigh Griffen."

Rhoda raised her brows expectantly. Ashleigh made eye contact with her and promptly forgot what to say.

"I can't do it!" Ashleigh cried as she tossed her report in the air. The papers rained down around her, but she didn't move to pick them up.

"Nonsense." Rhoda got off the bed and bent to pick up the report. "You can do anything you put your mind to. You just have to have faith in yourself." She glanced at the report. "I have to admit, I'm a little surprised at your choice of topics. Why ships? Do you know a lot about ships?"

Ashleigh shook her head. "I didn't know anything about them until I did the report."

Rhoda handed the report back to Ashleigh and walked over to the bookshelf on Ashleigh's side of the room. "That's a good way to learn new things," she said as she ran her finger over the spines of the books.

"But if you're trying to do something like learning to speak in front of an audience, you need to pick a topic you're comfortable with. One you know a lot about. And that would be . . . ?" She lifted a book on racehorses from the shelf.

"Horses!" Ashleigh said as she went over to the bookshelf herself and picked up a book on the great racehorse Man o' War.

"Exactly!" Rhoda smiled. "You're most comfortable when you're talking about horses, so why not do a report on something like managing a breeding farm or raising a racehorse? You wouldn't even need a book for that. It's something you help your parents with every day."

"Great idea!" Ashleigh cried. "That'll be easy."

"Well, not quite that easy," Rhoda said. "Once you've rewritten your report, you'll have to rehearse it in front of the mirror, and then in front of a live audience. We can use your family for that. But if you feel confident about your subject matter, I'm sure you'll give a great speech.

"By the way," Rhoda added with a smile, "I know your birthday is this Saturday. Anything special you'd like?"

Ashleigh grinned as she chose another horse book from her bookshelf. "The best present in the world would be if Aladdin won the Derby!"

Rhoda settled back on the bed with a worried frown. "I'll see what I can do."

Ashleigh couldn't wait to get home from school on Thursday. That afternoon she and Stardust would get to pony Aladdin all the way to the Wortons' farm! When she entered the barn, her parents already had the horses in the crossties and saddled.

"Mike's at the Wortons' waiting for you two," Mr. Griffen said. "He's decided to work out a schedule with Star Gazer's trainer."

Ashleigh accepted Stardust's reins from her mother, then mounted up and waited for Rhoda and Aladdin. The big colt shied to the side when Rhoda was given a leg up. Ashleigh noticed that Rhoda didn't put her feet immediately into the irons, but kept them tightly wrapped around Aladdin.

"Is something the matter with your stirrups?" Ashleigh asked as she slipped the leather strap through Aladdin's bit.

Rhoda knotted her reins and checked her equipment. "No, everything's fine. I'm not going to give him a chance to unbalance me today. He can do his jumping around now. When we're ready to work, I'll put my feet back in the irons."

Ashleigh moved the horses out onto the trail that

would take them to the Wortons' back fence.

"Is it okay to trot?"

"Sure," Rhoda said. "I did a lot of bareback riding as a kid. I can stay on like this."

Ashleigh asked Stardust for a trot, making sure to keep a good hold on Aladdin, who was fussing and tossing his head. If Ashleigh wasn't careful, she'd end up getting knocked out of the saddle.

At the first bounce of the trot, Aladdin gathered himself and tried to lunge forward, but Ashleigh was ready for him, keeping a steadying hand on the pony rein. The colt's ears flicked back and forth, listening to his rider as she moved in the rhythm of the trot.

"Get your mind on your business," Rhoda scolded, her expression serious. She shortened the reins. "We have only nine days till the Derby—we can't afford to goof off."

Ashleigh kept a tight hold on Aladdin as they crossed the big field. Several birds took flight, and each time the colt tucked his hindquarters and prepared to launch himself as though he were coming out of the starting gate.

Mike let them onto the Wortons' track. He ran a hand over Aladdin's damp coat. "Did you run this horse all the way here?"

Rhoda placed her hand on the colt's damp neck.

"All we did was a trot. He's just nervous. I can't get him to settle down."

Mike frowned. "Let's send him around the track a few times and see if that helps any." He made his way to a bench on the outside rail. "This is a six-furlong training track. Back him up to the finish line, them take him around twice," he instructed.

Rhoda put her feet in the irons and nodded to Ashleigh to turn her loose. She stood in the irons and took a short cross on the reins, crossing one rein over the other at the base of Aladdin's neck and grabbing the crossed section with both hands. "Easy, big guy," she said as she backtracked Aladdin at a trot toward the finish line.

Ashleigh got off Stardust and stood next to Mike, admiring the Wortons' new training track. White rails stood out in stark contrast to the green lawns, and a stand of elegant pine trees swayed in the breeze along the outer rail.

This is what Edgardale needs, Ashleigh thought dreamily, but she was jolted back to reality when she heard Mike's words of alarm.

"Hold him steady, Rhoda," Mike said when Aladdin ducked to the side at the large red-and-white striped finish pole.

Rhoda pulled Aladdin down to a walk and then

halted at the rail. Then she turned him and trotted off in the correct direction around the track to begin the workout.

Aladdin broke into a slow gallop, his ears moving forward and back as he took in the new surroundings. He jerked a few times when something startled him, but continued to move forward. When he reached Mike and Ashleigh, Aladdin spooked again, and Ashleigh could hear Rhoda's indrawn breath as the jockey tried to balance herself in the irons.

On the second time around, Mike leaned over the rail and yelled, "Pick up the speed, Rhoda! He needs a good gallop!"

Rhoda started to protest, but Mike signaled for her to go on.

They watched as Aladdin galloped around the oval, spooking here and there at a small tree or marker pole. He really wasn't acting like himself. After completing the run, Rhoda pulled Aladdin to a stop on the outside rail before making her way to the exit gate.

Aladdin pranced off the track with his neck arched, his coat gleaming with sweat. As they were passing through the gate, another horse galloped by on the inner rail. Aladdin tossed his head in the air and bolted. His hooves beat a rapid tattoo in the gravel, kicking up dirt and small rocks that pelted Mike and

Ashleigh. Rhoda hauled back on the reins, but Aladdin didn't stop until he reached the nearest barn.

Rhoda jumped down from Aladdin's back as Mike and Ashleigh hurried over. "I don't know what's gotten into him," she said, pulling the reins over Aladdin's head and leading him away from the barn.

Ashleigh could see that Rhoda's hands were shaking. "Here, let me take him," she offered as she mounted up on Stardust and prepared to loop the pony strap through Aladdin's bit.

"I've got him," Mike said. "Rhoda, you can catch a ride back to the barn with Ashleigh. I'll get Aladdin cleaned up and cooled out."

Ashleigh dismounted and handed Stardust's reins to Rhoda. "No, I want to stay. I can walk Aladdin back to Edgardale when Mike is finished," Ashleigh offered. "It isn't very far." Aladdin looked so on edge, she didn't want to leave the colt's side.

Rhoda pursed her lips and frowned. "I don't know if that's such a good idea, Ash. I'd hate to see you get hurt."

Ashleigh was shocked. Aladdin would never hurt her. He might have been a little spooky that day because of all the new sights and sounds at the Wortons' place, but he wasn't crazy.

Rhoda pulled the saddle from Aladdin's back and set it down on a rack. "Just be careful," she said. "He's already gotten away from us once. We don't need that to happen again. Aladdin might not be so lucky the next time."

She grabbed the cheek straps on Aladdin's bridle and looked into his eyes. "It's time for you to start acting like a Derby horse and not a low-class claimer. There's already one bad actor in the field," Rhoda said, referring to Star Gazer. "I don't want to be riding one, too."

Ashleigh glanced at Mike. She could tell by his raised eyebrows that he was surprised by Rhoda's outburst. Rhoda turned and mounted up on Stardust. "I'll see you back at the house, Ashleigh. Call if you need help getting Aladdin back to Edgardale."

"I want you to gallop Aladdin again on Saturday," Mike told her. "Ashleigh doesn't have school, so I'll meet you two here at eight in the morning, all right?"

Rhoda nodded hastily and turned Stardust toward Edgardale.

Ashleigh watched Rhoda canter Stardust across the field. Suddenly she felt very worried. What if Aladdin's manners didn't improve? And what if Rhoda didn't want to ride him in the Derby?

"Looks like our rider has a few concerns about Aladdin," Mike said as he walked the colt to the wash rack.

Ashleigh nodded as she held Aladdin for his bath.

She had thought she might be imagining the problem or blowing it out of proportion, but if Mike was noticing it, too . . .

"The sweat scraper is missing, Ash. Can you run into the barn and get one?" Mike asked.

Ashleigh walked into the large barn, looking down the long row of stalls. She spotted a wash bucket with a scraper sitting a couple of stalls away. When she reached for the scraper, she saw a sudden movement from the corner of her eye. She tried to jump out of the way but wasn't quick enough. She winced as a small bay horse pinned his ears and stretched his neck over the stall door, grazing her shoulder with his teeth.

Ashleigh rubbed her shoulder and glared at Star Gazer. She wanted to slap him on the end of the nose, but she didn't want to risk having his trainer see her do that. One of the grooms walked around the corner just then, and Ashleigh continued down the aisle, rubbing her shoulder as she went.

Before she left the barn, Ashleigh turned and made a face at Star Gazer. She would get her revenge when Aladdin beat him in the Kentucky Derby. If only she could help Rhoda and Aladdin work out their problems.

Ashleigh handed the scraper to Mike and held Aladdin's lead rope while he scraped the excess water from Aladdin's coat. As they were finishing, Zach Jackson walked up. Ashleigh was glad to see the jockey was back to riding after his fall from Go for Cover, but she was very surprised to see him at the Wortons' farm.

"What are you doing here, Zach?" Mike asked as he smiled a greeting.

Zach grinned and popped his whip smartly against his black riding boots. "Mr. Vargas offered me a ride aboard Star Gazer for the Derby. It's an offer I couldn't refuse."

Ashleigh heard Mike congratulate the jockey, but her heart sank. If Rhoda kept having problems with Aladdin, she might refuse to ride him. Zach Jackson would have been the next best choice. Now Zach wouldn't be available.

The Kentucky Derby was the next weekend, and things were looking worse and worse by the moment!

8

"Hey, birthday girl," Rhoda called as she threw back the covers. "Time to get out of bed."

Ashleigh slowly opened her eyes and glanced at the clock, then sat straight up in bed as her brain registered the time: 7:15 A.M. They had forty-five minutes before they were supposed to meet Mike at the Wortons'.

Rhoda pulled on her riding boots. "I'll see you at breakfast," she said, and headed downstairs.

Ashleigh slid her legs over the side of the bed. She was now eleven years old. Only five more years and she could get her jockey's license! She dressed quickly and went downstairs.

"Happy birthday, Ash," Mrs. Griffen said as she set a plate in front of Ashleigh and took her chair at the end of the table.

Ashleigh smiled. On her plate was a stack of pancakes with a candle sticking out of it.

"Hey, how come I don't get one of those?" Rory protested.

"Because it's not your birthday," Caroline said.

Ashleigh took the lighted candle and stuck it into Rory's toast. He smiled and blew out the candle. "I made a wish for you, Ash."

"I hope Aladdin won't be as spooky today as he was on Thursday," Mr. Griffen said.

Rhoda paused, setting her juice glass back on the table. "Yes, he *was* pretty bad the other day," Rhoda agreed. "I'm a little worried—Aladdin's not normally a spooky horse. We're only a week away from the Derby, and he's acting like a green, unbroken two-year-old. If he doesn't stop acting up, Mr. Danworth might want to reconsider paying that huge entry fee."

Ashleigh's breakfast lay like a brick in her stomach. Was Rhoda saying she thought Aladdin should be scratched? Ashleigh looked around the table to see if anybody else was worried about the way this conversation was going. Rory munched happily on his breakfast, but Caroline and Mrs. Griffen had stopped eating, and Mr. Griffen's brows were raised in disbelief.

Mr. Griffen cleared his throat. "Mike said he wants to try Aladdin in full-cup blinkers this morning. He thinks that might block out the scenery that's been spooking him."

Rhoda shrugged. "I hope it works. Blinkers usually help with a spooky horse, but Aladdin wasn't ever spooky until our accident."

Ashleigh's throat suddenly felt dry. She reached for her glass of milk. If Aladdin's jockey had already given up on him, they were in big trouble.

Rhoda set her fork down on her unfinished plate of eggs. "I'm going to head out to the barn and help Jonas put the mares out. I'll tack up Stardust and Aladdin while you finish eating, Ashleigh," Rhoda said as she looked at Ashleigh's half-eaten breakfast. Her chair scraped across the floor as she pushed back from the table. "I'll see you in a few minutes."

They waited until they heard the bang of the screen door before anyone spoke.

"We missed Aladdin's last workout," Mrs. Griffen said. "Is the colt really going that poorly?"

Ashleigh pushed her fork around on her plate, her appetite gone. She nodded. "He's been acting up a lot, and he keeps trying to run off."

Mr. Griffen got up from the table. "Well, let's hope these blinkers do the trick."

Ashleigh folded her napkin and stood up also, looking guiltily at her unfinished breakfast. "That was really good, Mom. Thanks," she said. Then she pulled on her riding boots and ran out the kitchen door.

When Ashleigh got to the barn, Rhoda was leading

Stardust outside. She mounted up, laughing when the chestnut mare walked right to Aladdin's side. "You kind of like this ponying stuff, don't you, girl? Maybe Mike will use you in the Derby to keep Aladdin calm."

Ashleigh patted the mare on the neck, imagining all the flowers and ribbons she could use to decorate Stardust if she was to pony in the Derby.

"You'd better get going," Mr. Griffen said. "Mike will meet you there with the blinkers. The rest of us are driving over in the car."

Ashleigh leaned in to put the lead strap on Aladdin. Rhoda sat like a statue on the colt's back. She looked really nervous.

Aladdin fussed, moving his hindquarters away from Stardust and pushing the mare with his shoulder. Stardust cocked her leg in warning, and Ashleigh gasped in surprise. She hadn't counted on Stardust trying to kick the colt. "Straighten up, you," Ashleigh scolded as she gave Stardust a small jerk on the reins. They had enough problems without worrying about Stardust injuring Aladdin. Rhoda remained quiet, gripping the reins with white-knuckled fists.

Ashleigh moved the horses down the trail, trying to think of something to break the silence.

"My teacher okayed my horse speech yesterday, and I've practiced it a couple of times in front of the mirror," Ashleigh said. "But I still get nervous. How am I going to speak in front of my whole class when I have trouble speaking in front of myself?"

Rhoda relaxed and turned her attention to Ashleigh. "You just have to have confidence in yourself. You don't worry when you're riding Stardust, do you?"

"No," Ashleigh said, not seeing a connection.

"That's because you know you can do it. You have to gain that same confidence in speaking. The more you practice, the better you'll do. You should give your speech in front of your family tonight."

"But it's my birthday," Ashleigh protested.

"The more pressure, the better." Rhoda laughed. "You can do it just before you cut the birthday cake."

Ashleigh turned her attention back to the horses, surprised that Aladdin hadn't pulled any tricks while they were talking. She glanced at Rhoda, noting how calm she seemed. Why was everything back to normal all of a sudden?

Up ahead, the Wortons' big white barn loomed. Mike was waiting for them at the end of the trail.

"There's Mike with the blinkers," Rhoda said. She straightened her posture and fidgeted with the reins.

Aladdin fought the pressure on his mouth and began sidestepping and tossing his head. He bumped Stardust with his hip, and Ashleigh felt the mare give in to the bigger horse. She put her heel into Stardust's side, asking the mare to push back. "Come on,

Aladdin," she said as she pulled his head toward her. "You were behaving so well a moment ago."

Ashleigh pulled to a stop in front of the trainer and waited while he put the blinkers on Aladdin.

"Let's do the same routine we tried on Thursday," Mike said to Rhoda. "Only this time I want Ashleigh to backtrack you to the finish line, then turn you loose. That'll give Aladdin a little time to get used to these blinkers," Mike said as he fastened them on Aladdin's head. "Aladdin's only worn blinkers a couple of times, and they didn't stay over his eyes very long," he said as he grinned at Ashleigh, reminding her of her beach gallop on Aladdin a couple of months earlier. "Gallop him twice around," Mike instructed, and turned them loose.

Rhoda nodded, but seemed nervous.

"I take it Aladdin didn't go very well in blinkers last time," Rhoda said.

"I got bucked off," Ashleigh said, then immediately regretted her words when she saw the worried look on Rhoda's face.

"I hope it works better this time," Rhoda said grimly. She tightened the strap on her helmet and double-checked the girth.

They entered the track, and Ashleigh asked Stardust for a brisk trot. Aladdin strode out at their side, with Rhoda posting in time to his rhythm. Aladdin kept turning his head, trying to see around the full-cup blinkers. The new equipment limited what the colt saw, but he seemed twice as surprised when something came into his line of vision. He kept his head up and his neck rigid, snorting loudly.

They reached the finish line, and Ashleigh pulled the leather strap through Aladdin's bit. "You're on your own, Rhoda. Good luck," she said as she made her way back to Mike.

Rhoda made Aladdin stand for a few moments, then turned and trotted him off. Aladdin balked at first but soon moved slowly down the track. The gallop seemed to go well until the first red-and-white quarter pole, when Aladdin shifted so fast to the side, he almost lost his rider.

Ashleigh's heart sank when Zach Jackson entered the track on Star Gazer. She glanced at Mike and saw that he was scowling. The trainers had agreed not to work their horses at the same time, but Star Gazer's trainer wasn't holding up his end of the deal.

Aladdin was almost around to the finish line, putting half a track between the two horses. But Zach was asking the little bay colt for a fast gallop. At that pace, Star Gazer would soon catch up to Aladdin.

Ashleigh gritted her teeth. Whenever Star Gazer was around, trouble was sure to follow. She kept her eyes on Aladdin, holding her breath every time the big colt spooked at something new.

"It doesn't look like the blinkers are helping very much," Mike said. He ran a hand over his eyes and sighed. "I'm at wit's end with this colt. These blinkers were my last hope for a quick fix."

Ashleigh shaded her eyes, following Aladdin's progress around the turn. "Maybe it'll just take him a while to get used to them."

"Yes, but we've only got a week until the Derby. He should be going better than this," Mike said. "We're running out of time."

Aladdin came out of the turn, heading into his second circuit around the track. Rhoda held him to a slow gallop in the center of the course. The big colt switched leads several times as he bent his head, looking for distractions.

Ashleigh kept an eye on Star Gazer. At the pace he was traveling, he would catch up to Aladdin at the top of the homestretch. She saw Aladdin's ears flick back to catch the sound of Star Gazer's galloping hooves.

Ashleigh had a sinking feeling in her stomach. Even from there, she could tell that Aladdin wasn't paying attention to his rider. When Star Gazer was four lengths off Aladdin's tail, she saw the black colt throw his head into the air and try to bolt.

Ashleigh clutched the rail, feeling as though she were in the saddle with Rhoda as the jockey fought for control of the colt. Rhoda hauled on the reins, keeping Aladdin's head bowed so he couldn't run away, but it didn't stop him from ducking and diving, zigzagging right and then left down the track.

Aladdin propped hard, slamming all four feet into the ground for a fraction of a second before he continued on. Rhoda lost her balance and started to head over Aladdin's right shoulder, but the colt spooked again and jumped back under her.

Ashleigh held her breath as Rhoda regained her balance and Aladdin shot to the outside rail. Rhoda stood straight up in the stirrups and cranked Aladdin's head right into the rail.

Ashleigh's heart leaped into her throat. "What's she doing?" she cried. "Does she want him to run into the rail?"

Mike squinted to see what was happening, using his hat to shade his eyes against the sun's glare. "She's trying to slow him down, but Aladdin can't see the rail with those blinkers on. Rhoda's got to turn his head so he can see the fence, or he'll run through it."

Ashleigh couldn't imagine the courage it would take to turn a running horse, especially one that was spooking, toward a solid rail. Aladdin looked as if he would be more likely to hit the rail than stop.

Aladdin did stop when he saw the fence, digging his front hooves into the track. It was more like a western sliding stop than a proper halt, and Rhoda was thrown forward onto the colt's neck.

Rhoda waited until Star Gazer passed by them once more, then she turned Aladdin and walked him back to the track exit. Mike stepped out to grab Aladdin as he came off the track, but Aladdin shied away.

When Mike had a solid hold on Aladdin's reins, Rhoda took her feet out of the irons and unsnapped her chin strap. The jockey's face was colorless except for two big blotches of red over her cheeks, and her breathing was shallow and rapid.

"What happened?" Mike asked as he pulled the blinkers from Aladdin's head.

"The same thing that's been happening all week, only worse!" Rhoda exclaimed. "I really thought we had a chance to prove ourselves in the Derby, but this horse has gone over the edge. He'll never be able to run like this. I think you should call Mr. Danworth and tell him to scratch Aladdin from the Derby."

Ashleigh gasped as all the air seemed to rush out of her lungs. Scratch Aladdin? They couldn't! They just had to figure out what was wrong, that was all.

She looked at Mike, panic taking hold of her. The trainer frowned, as if he actually believed that Rhoda might be right.

This couldn't be happening—Ashleigh had to do something!

9

Ashleigh stabbed the pitchfork into the bedding in Stardust's stall and tossed the soiled straw into the wheelbarrow. What a rotten birthday this had turned out to be. She heard footsteps coming down the barn aisle, but she ignored them. She didn't feel like talking to anyone.

Rhoda stopped in the open stall doorway. "I'm sorry, Ashleigh. I don't know if I'm going to be able to give you your birthday wish," she said, forcing a smile. "There's nothing I want more than to win the Kentucky Derby on Aladdin, but he's just not cooperating. He's got some real problems."

Ashleigh continued to muck out the stall, trying to swallow the lump that was rising in her throat. She wanted to tell Rhoda that she couldn't give up, but she was afraid that if she spoke, she might start to cry.

"Ashleigh?" Rhoda stepped closer. "Don't cry. Nobody

should cry on their birthday. Here, let me get you a tissue." She walked back down the aisle, her shoulders slumped in sympathy.

Ashleigh counted the receding footsteps. *Two ... one ... four ... eight ... What can I do?* she wondered desperately. She couldn't let Rhoda give up on Aladdin. He had proven once that he could win with Rhoda aboard. He could do it again, she was sure of it.

She set the pitchfork in the corner and dashed out of the stall, knocking over the wheelbarrow in the process. "Rhoda, wait!" she called as she ran down the aisle.

Rhoda stopped and turned. "What is it, Ashleigh?"

"I changed my wish," Ashleigh announced between breaths.

Rhoda tilted her head. "Changed it to what?"

Ashleigh looped her arm through Rhoda's, walking her out to the paddock where Aladdin stood cropping grass. She wiped at the tears that had pooled in her eyes and tried to smile. "I know Aladdin can win the Kentucky Derby with you riding him. You've done better with him than any other jockey. But I'm not going to ask you to win the race, like I did before." Ashleigh glanced at Rhoda to see if she had her attention. "I don't care if he wins. Just let him run."

Ashleigh could see the doubt in Rhoda's eyes. She knew she'd have to throw something bigger into the deal to make Rhoda agree. "Look, you've been helping me with my oral report. You told me that I just need to have confidence in myself. If I promise to rehearse a lot and stand up in front of that class with confidence on Monday morning, will you promise to ride Aladdin in the Derby?"

Rhoda let out a big sigh. "You make a pretty good negotiator, Ash." She gave Ashleigh an affectionate slug on the shoulder. "You're right. We should keep trying. This day is almost over, but as of tomorrow, we've still got six days till post time. Maybe things will work out."

Ashleigh threw her arms around the jockey. "Thanks, Rhoda! You won't regret this!"

Just then Aladdin snorted loudly and scooted off, tearing across the grass like a wild stallion.

"I'm not so sure about that," Rhoda said, watching the colt intently.

"Make a wish and blow out the candles, Ashleigh," Rory said as he poked his finger into the icing on the side of the cake.

Ashleigh knew exactly what she wanted to wish for. She took a deep breath and blew out the eleven candles. Everyone clapped.

"Here's your first present," Mrs. Griffen said, handing Ashleigh a foil-wrapped package with a pink ribbon. It was from Caroline.

Ashleigh tore into it. "Wow!" she said as she lifted the pretty peach-colored dress out of the box. Ashleigh had never liked dresses, but this one was simple and looked as though it would suit her.

"It's for the race, Ash," Caroline said. "I knew we'd never get you in a dress for school, but the Kentucky Derby is going to be really special this year."

Ashleigh's eyes darted around the room, catching the sympathetic looks on everyone's faces that said they knew how close Aladdin was to not making it to the Derby.

Ashleigh hugged her sister. "Thanks, Caro. It's beautiful."

"Here, Ash, open mine," Mona said as she handed her friend a large, flat present wrapped in paper with horses running on it.

Ashleigh tore off the paper and discovered the bright blue saddle pad she had been admiring in the local saddle shop. "Thanks so much, Mona. Stardust will love this."

By the time Ashleigh had opened all her gifts, she had several new articles of clothing, some new riding boots, the blue saddle pad, and a blue-and-white cover for her helmet.

"Thanks, everybody," Ashleigh said as she stuffed a piece of cake into her mouth.

"Not so fast," Rhoda said. "There's one more gift left, but I believe you told me you were going to give a speech to everyone first."

A piece of cake lodged in her throat, and Ashleigh coughed. She looked at all the expectant faces surrounding her. *I really don't want to do this,* she thought. None of her classmates expected her to be able to give a good speech, anyway—why should she even bother?

But then Ashleigh caught sight of Aladdin's first win photo hanging on their wall, and she remembered how she was the only one who had believed he could win. She hadn't given up on him, and then he'd proved himself and won.

She couldn't give up on herself, either.

Ashleigh took a big gulp of milk and cleared her throat. Then she stood and faced the group. "'Managing a Breeding Farm,' by Ashleigh Griffen . . ."

The speech passed in a blur, but everyone clapped when she was finished. She had actually done it! She hoped it was going to be this easy on Monday.

Then Rhoda held up a small box with a ribbon on it. "This is for you," she said, and handed the box to Ashleigh.

Ashleigh carefully opened the box, her mouth dropping open when she saw what lay inside. It was a small silver charm of a horse and jockey on a delicate necklace.

"It's for good luck," Rhoda said.

"Thanks!" Ashleigh handed the box to her mother and lifted her hair so Mrs. Griffen could fasten the necklace around her throat. "I love it."

Rhoda smiled modestly and picked up her plate of cake, finishing it off.

They spent the rest of the night playing card games and watching videos of some of Ashleigh's favorite races. Before she went to bed, Ashleigh grabbed a handful of carrots and a big piece of chocolate cake and headed for the barn.

There was a light on in the tack room when Ashleigh opened the barn door. She found Jonas sitting in a chair, oiling some leather halters. He smiled when she came in.

"Happy birthday, Ashleigh," Jonas said. He wiped his hands on his overalls and accepted the plate of chocolate cake. "I'm sorry I didn't make it up to the house for your birthday dinner, but it took me longer in town than I thought. I didn't want to interrupt in the middle."

"That's all right," Ashleigh said. "I just wanted to make sure you got a piece of cake before it was all gone. I'll see you in the morning."

Ashleigh went to Stardust's stall and leaned over the door. Stardust pushed her nose into Ashleigh's hair and whuffed softly. Ashleigh laughed. "That tickles." She rubbed the mare's forehead and kissed her on the tip of the nose. Stardust shook her head and blew through her lips. "See, it does tickle, doesn't it?" she said with a giggle.

Ashleigh dug the carrots out of her pocket and fed them to Stardust. "You know, Aladdin's been acting funny, and Rhoda doesn't like riding him. No one thinks Aladdin's any good anymore." She threw her arms around the mare's neck. "Oh, Stardust, I've got to figure out what's wrong with Aladdin," Ashleigh cried.

Stardust stood quietly as Ashleigh poured out her worries. Finally Ashleigh kissed her mare good night and headed back to the house to go to bed.

The next day Rhoda would gallop Aladdin again.

Ashleigh jumped out of bed when the alarm went off.

"Come on, Rhoda. It's time to get up," she said, pulling on her jeans.

A grumble came from the other bed.

"Rhoda?"

"Leave me alone," Rhoda pleaded, and drew the covers over her head.

"But it's morning. You're going to gallop Aladdin

today," Ashleigh said, pulling on her socks.

Rhoda groaned. "I don't feel very well. I think it's the flu."

Ashleigh paused in the middle of tying her shoes. "But you have to get up. Who else will ride Aladdin?"

Rhoda pulled the covers over her head. "Try Zach Jackson. He's over at the Wortons' place anyway."

Ashleigh sat on the bed, speechless. Rhoda rolled over, presenting her with her back—a good indication that she had no intention of getting up and going to work.

Ashleigh made her way downstairs to the kitchen. "Rhoda's sick," she said to her mother and father. "She won't be down to gallop Aladdin."

"Well, there's nothing we can do about it if she's not feeling well," Mr. Griffen said as he finished off his coffee and placed the cup in the sink. "Maybe Zach can gallop Aladdin today. It might be nice to have another opinion on him." He glanced at his watch. "Mike should be at the Wortons' by now. I'll call the barn and tell him what's happened."

Ashleigh followed her mother down to the barn while her father called Mike.

"If Rhoda has the flu, I hope it's just the twenty-four-hour kind," Mrs. Griffen said. She carried Stardust's saddle and bridle from the tack room while Ashleigh led the mare from her stall. "Aladdin will need a few more gallops in him before the Derby." She haltered Aladdin and snapped him into the second set of crossties just as Mr. Griffen came into the barn.

"You might as well put him away," Mr. Griffen said, gesturing to Aladdin. "Mike made a quick call to Mr. Danworth, and Mr. Danworth said he didn't want anyone else on Aladdin before the Derby, especially the jockey for the Derby favorite," he said, alluding to Zach. "According to Mike, Rhoda signed a contract with the Danworths saying that until the Derby she would ride Aladdin exclusively."

"Why?" Mrs. Griffen asked.

Mr. Griffen pulled an empty hay net from the nearest stall and tossed it in front of the hay stack. "That type of contract isn't unheard of," he said. "The Danworths just want to protect their interest. If Rhoda were to keep working with other horses, she could get hurt. Then Mike would end up having to hire another rider; someone who didn't know Aladdin as well as Rhoda. That could hurt his chances in the Derby.

"But that contract works both ways," Mr. Griffen went on. "The Danworths can't put another rider on Aladdin unless Rhoda is injured badly enough that she can't ride."

Ashleigh turned that information over in her mind. In a way it was good news. Rhoda couldn't back out of riding Aladdin unless he was scratched from the race.

But she could still convince Mike that Aladdin should be scratched.

Ashleigh pulled off Stardust's tack and turned her out into the side paddock. She could get her chores out of the way now that Aladdin had the day off, but first she stopped by the black colt's stall. She didn't want him to feel neglected.

Aladdin stepped eagerly to the front of his stall, blowing softly against Ashleigh's hair. She stroked his soft muzzle and looked into his intelligent brown eyes. "What's your secret?" she whispered. "Why don't you run well for Rhoda anymore? It's been a while since the accident. You're not holding that against her, are you?"

Aladdin nuzzled Ashleigh's face, then pushed on her shoulder. "I know what you're looking for," Ashleigh said as she pulled half a carrot from her pocket and fed it to him.

Aladdin chewed the carrot and then nuzzled her hands for more. Ashleigh tugged on his silky black ears. He was such a sweet horse. Why didn't Rhoda like him anymore?

Ashleigh helped her mother finish the stalls, then returned to the house to check on Rhoda. She took the stairs to the bedroom two at a time, but when she opened her bedroom door, the room was empty and Rhoda's bed had been made.

Ashleigh frowned. Where was Rhoda? She went back down the stairs, cutting to the kitchen to grab a glass of water. She stopped dead in her tracks at the sight of the jockey sitting at the kitchen table eating a big plate of bacon and eggs.

The guilty look on Rhoda's face told Ashleigh that the jockey's illness had been a ruse. "I thought you were sick!" Ashleigh accused.

She waited for an explanation.

Rhoda swallowed hard, her eyes moving around the old farmhouse kitchen, never landing on Ashleigh. "I'm feeling much better now. But I'm going back to bed as soon as I'm through here."

Ashleigh felt sick at heart. Rhoda had lied to her.

Rhoda's not planning to ride Aladdin in the Derby at all, is she?

10

Ashleigh turned and walked out of the kitchen, her heart heavy with the jockey's betrayal. Rhoda was supposed to be her friend, but friends didn't lie to each other. She left the house, heading back out to the barn. What she needed was a good gallop on Stardust. That always made her feel better.

Her mother was cleaning out water buckets in the wash stall. She turned off the hose.

"How's Rhoda doing?" she asked.

"She's sleeping," Ashleigh answered, staring at the ground. She didn't want to look her mother in the eye for fear she would see Rhoda's betrayal written there. Ashleigh wasn't sure why, but she didn't want to tell her parents about finding Rhoda at the breakfast table.

She grabbed Stardust's halter and brought the mare back from the pasture, hooking her into the crossties. She poured her frustration with Rhoda into her grooming, brushing Stardust's coat until she shone like a show horse. Then she placed her new blue saddle pad on Stardust's back and slid the saddle into place. She reached for the bridle and sighed as she untangled it. She couldn't really blame Rhoda if she was afraid to ride Aladdin. The jockey had taken a pretty nasty fall, and Aladdin had been hard to ride ever since.

She pulled the bridle over Stardust's ears and led her out of the barn. It was a beautiful spring day and the birds were singing, but Ashleigh didn't feel very cheerful. It was bad enough that Aladdin's entry in the Derby was in doubt, but to make matters worse, the next day was Monday, and she would have to give her oral report.

Ashleigh mounted up and pressed Stardust into a walk. When they reached the edge of the property, Ashleigh started reciting her oral report again.

Stardust's ears flicked back and forth at the sound of Ashleigh's voice. Ashleigh ran through her speech over and over, starting over when she made a mistake or forgot where she was. When she had gone through it twice in a row without any major mistakes, she stopped. Her speech was as good as it was going to get.

She looked around and discovered that she had ridden to the field with the large stumps where she and Stardust had first tried jumping. She wondered if the fallen trees that they had practiced on were still there.

Ashleigh hadn't jumped in a while, but she thought it might be fun to pop over the two-foot jump just once.

She rode to the area with the fallen trees, but she was disappointed. Somebody had cut them up for firewood. There was another downed tree a little further away, but it was about three and a half feet off the ground.

Stardust pricked her ears in anticipation when they approached the log, but Ashleigh wasn't so sure. It looked awfully high, and it was so solid. She walked Stardust around it several times, trying to decide what she wanted to do. "What do you think, girl?" she asked the mare. "Do you want to try it?"

She trotted Stardust some distance up the field and then turned back to the jump, asking her for a canter as they approached the log. Stardust cantered steadily forward, eager to make the jump. But the closer they got, the bigger the jump looked to Ashleigh, and she pulled the mare to a halt just a stride before takeoff.

Stardust shook her mane and blew through her nostrils as Ashleigh turned her away from the jump. "What's the matter, girl? Were you looking forward to that?" Ashleigh felt a little guilty. Jumping hadn't been her favorite thing, but Stardust had loved it. She looked back at the log again and shrugged. If Stardust wanted to jump it, she might as well try.

Ashleigh trotted her mare back to the starting

place, glancing back at the jump several times. *You can do this,* she told herself, trying to keep her hands steady on the reins, but she could feel them shaking as she urged Stardust into a canter.

Stardust cantered toward the jump, but the strong, confident manner she'd had minutes before was gone. She tossed her head and cantered sideways. Ashleigh straightened her out and aimed her toward the log. Her heart beat faster as they moved closer and closer to the jump. Ashleigh leaned forward for takeoff, but Stardust slammed on the brakes, cutting hard to the left to avoid crashing into the downed tree.

Ashleigh held on with all her might, staying with Stardust as she turned sharply and came to a stop. "I thought you wanted to jump," she said in surprise. Ashleigh was dumbfounded. When they'd first seen the jump, Stardust gave her all the signals that said she wanted to take it. What had changed her mind?

Ashleigh circled the mare as she waited for her heartbeat to return to normal. She looked down at her shaking hands, and it dawned on her what the problem might be. Her mother and father had always told her that a rider could telegraph her fear to a horse through her hands and body signals.

Ashleigh had been confident about jumping until they got closer to the log, and then she'd chickened out altogether. When they tried the second time,

Ashleigh had been scared. And that was when Stardust had begun to run sideways and refused the jump.

To test her theory, Ashleigh walked Stardust into a cleared area of the field. She trotted a figure eight and cantered a circle. These were exercises they did almost every time she rode—exercises she was confident they could do.

Stardust behaved perfectly. When Ashleigh showed confidence, so did her horse.

Maybe that's Rhoda's problem, Ashleigh thought as she turned her mare for home. She knew Rhoda was afraid of Aladdin, but she had assumed that fear was caused by Aladdin's bad behavior. But maybe it was the other way around. Aladdin was acting up because Rhoda was afraid!

Maybe there wasn't anything wrong with Aladdin at all.

Ashleigh wasn't sure how she was going to test this theory, since nobody else was allowed to ride Aladdin, but she promised herself she'd find a way. She had to. Too much was at stake.

Ashleigh cantered most of the way home, pulling Stardust down to a walk when she entered the stable area. She was anxious to see if Rhoda was still playing sick or if she had decided to ride Aladdin after all.

Ashleigh gave Stardust a good brushing, then turned her out in the paddock. She headed for the house and went straight to her room. Rhoda was sitting on the bed.

Ashleigh couldn't think of any other way to phrase her feelings, so she just came right out and said it. "I know you were pretending to be sick this morning because you're afraid of Aladdin. Please don't give up on him, Rhoda. I know he's got some problems, but you can work them out. You have to."

Rhoda drew her legs up and propped her chin on top of her knees. "I'm really sorry I lied to you this morning, Ash. You didn't deserve that. I don't know what's come over me." She took a deep breath and sighed. "Ever since I was a little girl, I always dreamed of riding in the Kentucky Derby. And now I've got this great opportunity and a terrific horse to ride, but something's happened and I feel like my dream is slipping away. I've been very lucky. But what about the next time? I'm afraid to ride Aladdin, Ashleigh."

Ashleigh nodded in sympathy. She remembered the fear she had felt only an hour before, when she and Stardust had approached that jump. "Maybe if we go try Aladdin right now, we can figure something out," Ashleigh suggested.

Rhoda gave her a weak smile. "Not today, Ashleigh. Mike called just after you left for your ride. He wants us to take Aladdin out on the trails tomorrow after you get home from school, then I'm supposed to breeze him on Thursday. The Danworths are flying in for that." Rhoda paused and took a deep breath. "Mike had to tell them about Aladdin's acting up. If Aladdin doesn't turn in a good performance on Thursday, they're going to scratch him from the Derby."

Ashleigh sucked in her breath. They had to fix Aladdin's problem by Thursday! She knew that Mr. Danworth was a smart businessman and wouldn't leave Aladdin in the race on the hope of a last-minute miracle.

"Can't we . . . ," Ashleigh faltered.

Rhoda shook her head. "Is it okay if we don't talk about this anymore? I really do feel a headache coming on now," Rhoda said. She rubbed her temples, her expression pained.

Ashleigh sighed. She didn't like seeing Rhoda feel this bad. They sat for a moment in companionable silence, then Ashleigh spoke up, trying to change the subject to something besides horses. "I've got to give my speech tomorrow," she said

"You'll do fine," Rhoda assured her. "Let's hear your report once more. Stand at the foot of the bed and pretend I'm your whole class. We'll go over it as many times as you need to."

That night, when they turned out the lights, Ashleigh really did feel confident about her speech. If only Rhoda felt the same confidence about Aladdin!

"You did it, Ash. You actually did it!" Mona said as they stepped off the school bus Monday afternoon. She slapped Ashleigh a high five. "You were great!"

Ashleigh glowed with her praise. "I made a few mistakes, and I stuttered a couple of times, but my report did turn out pretty well, didn't it?" she admitted. "I can't wait to tell Rhoda. She really helped me a lot." Ashleigh adjusted her book bag and looked out over the pastures of grazing mares and foals. She wished she could help Rhoda the way the jockey had helped her. But what could she do?

She said good-bye to Mona at the end of Edgardale's long driveway and ran all the way home. She entered the house with a bang of the screen door and took the steps two at a time. Rhoda was sitting on the bed polishing her tall black riding boots.

"I did it, Rhoda," Ashleigh said as she pulled her book bag off her shoulder and flung it onto the bed. "I got an A on my oral report, and it's all thanks to you."

"That's great, Ashleigh," Rhoda said. "I knew you could do it!"

Ashleigh quickly changed into jeans and a riding shirt. "Are you ready to take Aladdin out?" Ashleigh could feel the jockey hesitate. "I'll be riding Stardust. We can pony you through all the trails. It'll be safer that way."

Rhoda held the boots up to the light for inspection. "You go on ahead, Ash. I'll be down in a few minutes."

Ashleigh went to the barn to saddle the horses. Jonas got Aladdin and put him in the crossties while Ashleigh tacked up Stardust. Rhoda showed up a few minutes later and leaned on the barn door while Jonas finished saddling Aladdin.

"Can I go with you, Ash?" Rory said, running down the barn aisle with his riding helmet on. "Moe can keep up. I can ride him fast now."

Ashleigh giggled at the thought of Moe trying to keep up with Aladdin. "Sorry, Rory. This is a work-out for Aladdin. We have to go by ourselves." She unsnapped Stardust from the crossties. "I thought Mom was giving you a lesson today."

Rory smiled. "She is, but I think it would be more fun to ride with the big horses."

Ashleigh and Rhoda laughed as they led the horses down the aisle. Rory was definitely following in her footsteps, Ashleigh thought. She had given Moe to Rory when she had outgrown the pony. Now Rory was waiting to get his saddle on Stardust.

Aladdin fidgeted nervously when Rhoda mounted up, but he settled down a bit when Ashleigh moved in and pulled the pony strap through his bit.

Rhoda knotted her reins as she rode alongside

Ashleigh. "What do you want to do today?"

Ashleigh bumped Stardust up to a trot, and Aladdin matched the pace. "How about if we go try Jessica's Jump?" she joked, trying to relieve the tension she saw building in Rhoda's face.

Rhoda's head snapped around. "You wouldn't really try that, would you?"

Ashleigh shrugged. "Mona and I have jumped the smaller end of it, but it's not very wide or deep there. It's just a normal creek."

Rhoda pulled Aladdin back to a walk. "With everything that can go wrong on a horse, it's easy enough to get hurt. There's no sense looking for trouble."

Ashleigh asked Stardust for a brisk trot, and Aladdin fell into step with her. "I know it would be crazy to ever try such a big jump, but wouldn't it be cool to be the first person to make it?"

Rhoda shook her head in exasperation and rolled her eyes. "I'm going to pretend I didn't hear that."

"Are you ready for a canter?" Ashleigh asked when they reached the wide part of the trail. When Rhoda nodded, Ashleigh asked Stardust to quicken her pace, and she took a tight hold on Aladdin's strap.

Ashleigh was pleased that Aladdin picked up the easy gait, but his ears flicked back and forth as he eyed the tall grass at the edge of the trail, looking for any movement. He switched leads several times to duck away from suspicious-looking bushes, but Rhoda stayed with him.

After a mile of cantering they pulled the horses down to a trot and continued for another mile. When they reached the field with Jessica's Jump they settled into a walk, lengthening their reins to let their horses stretch their necks.

"Well, I've survived the ride so far," Rhoda said.

Ashleigh knew Rhoda's comment was meant as a joke, but she could tell Rhoda was nervous just being up on Aladdin's back.

"Do you want to head back?" Ashleigh asked as she let Stardust drop her head to crop the grass.

Rhoda looked out over the grassy field. Aladdin tried to stretch his head down, but the pony strap stopped him. "Maybe we should let them eat for a while," Rhoda said. "Aladdin always seems to relax when he gets to eat. Just pull the pony strap through the bit so he can reach the ground."

"Will you be okay?" Ashleigh waited for Rhoda's nod before she pulled the strap clear of Aladdin's bit. She worried that if the big horse sensed he was no longer attached, he might decide to take off, but Aladdin stayed where he was, happily cropping the rich Kentucky bluegrass.

Ashleigh leaned back in her saddle and breathed in

the wonderful smells of spring. Meadow flowers were blooming everywhere, and the scents of pine and freshly cropped grass lingered on the breeze. She looked at Aladdin standing a few feet away with the sun glinting off his jet black coat. He looked so peaceful.

"We should probably be heading home." Rhoda's voice broke the silence. "Your mom will have dinner on the table pretty soon."

Ashleigh nodded and pulled Stardust's head up, but the mare fought the bit, trying to lower her muzzle back to the grass.

Rhoda walked Aladdin to Stardust's side, waiting for Ashleigh to put on the pony strap. "Looks like she's not full yet." Rhoda chuckled.

"Come on, Stardust," Ashleigh said as she pulled harder on the reins. Stardust lifted her head and pinned her ears at Aladdin. "Hey, it's not his fault," Ashleigh scolded as she slipped the pony strap back through Aladdin's bit. "Sometimes she gets a little cranky," Ashleigh apologized.

They circled the horses toward home. A bird flew up in front of them, and Aladdin pressed close to Stardust, nervously chewing on his bit. Ashleigh was surprised as the reins jerked out of her hands and her mare took a nip at the big colt.

"Stardust!" Ashleigh growled, pulling the mare's head around. But Aladdin pinned his ears and returned the bite, snapping at Stardust's shoulder.

"Watch it!" Rhoda hollered as she reined Aladdin in.

Stardust squealed, her ears pinned flat against her head, and Ashleigh felt the mare's hindquarters rise as she kicked out at Aladdin, barely missing him.

Aladdin ran sideways, trying to get away from the temperamental mare.

Ashleigh held tight to the strap, but Aladdin was just too strong. She cried out as she felt the leather strap sliding through her fingers. The big stallion continued to run sideways until the leather ran completely through Ashleigh's hand and he was free of Stardust.

"Whoa!" Rhoda hollered, but the big horse would hear none of it. He threw his head up, trying to loosen the jockey's grip on the reins.

Ashleigh ran forward with Stardust, hoping to reach out and grab the flapping pony strap, but Aladdin just ran faster.

"Reach in and grab the strap!" Rhoda yelled. "I don't think I can hold him. He's going to run away with me."

Ashleigh urged Stardust to go faster as they cut across the meadow. She tried to lean in and catch the strap, but the big black Thoroughbred snorted and took off as though he were in a race.

Rhoda stood in the stirrups and hauled back on the

reins with all her might. But Aladdin wouldn't slow down, and there was no way Stardust could keep up with him.

As they approached the middle of the field, Ashleigh's heart stopped. Aladdin was heading straight for Jessica's Jump! She had to warn Rhoda!

"Come on, Stardust," she said as she pumped her hands up and down her mare's neck, asking for all of her speed. "Rhoda!" she screamed. "Rhoda, look out for the creek!" She could see Rhoda tugging on Aladdin's left rein, trying to turn the colt from his headlong flight, but Aladdin didn't budge from his course.

Ashleigh could hear nothing but her heart pounding in her chest as she watched Rhoda and Aladdin race closer and closer to the creek. There was no way they could make it over that part of the water. It was too far across. Rhoda continued to pull on the reins, trying to turn Aladdin, but it wasn't working. Ashleigh reined her mare in.

In another moment it was going to be too late for Rhoda and Aladdin. "Jump off!" Ashleigh yelled when she realized that Aladdin couldn't be turned. "Rhoda, you've got to get off!"

Ashleigh could see Rhoda looking down at the ground on both sides of her horse, then straight ahead at the deep cut in the earth where the creek flowed. They were almost upon it. Ashleigh held her breath, then gasped as Rhoda leaped from Aladdin's back, tumbling over and over in the tall grass.

Aladdin continued ahead for a few more strides, then cut hard to the right, circling in a big arc, and jetted off across the fields toward the tree line.

Ashleigh cantered over to where Rhoda lay, flying out of the saddle before Stardust even came to a complete stop. "Are you okay?" Ashleigh cried as she helped the shaken jockey to her feet.

Rhoda stood, brushing the grass and dirt from her clothes and testing her bones for breaks. "My head hurts, but I—I think I'm okay," she stammered. "How's Aladdin?"

They stared off across the meadow to where Aladdin was just disappearing into the forest.

"It looks like he's running okay," Ashleigh said as she put her hand to her eyes, trying to separate the colt from the shadows. "But we'd better catch him quick."

Rhoda wiped her hand across her brow, and Ashleigh sucked in her breath. Blood!

"You're hurt!" Ashleigh grabbed Rhoda's hand and looked for a cut, but couldn't see one. "It's your head!" Ashleigh gasped as she saw a trickle of blood run down Rhoda's forehead.

"You've got to get back to Edgardale," Ashleigh said as she handed Stardust's reins to Rhoda.

But the jockey shook her head and refused to take the reins. "I can't leave a Derby horse out running wild in the forest."

"I'll catch him," Ashleigh said.

Rhoda looked at Ashleigh and frowned. "I can't leave you out here, either!" Several drops of blood rolled down Rhoda's face and dropped onto her shirt.

Ashleigh scowled. "I don't know much about first aid, but I do know that a head wound can be dangerous. You need to get back to Edgardale and call the doctor! You fell really hard when you jumped."

Ashleigh could tell by the skeptical look on Rhoda's bloodstained face that she wasn't convinced. "Please," Ashleigh pleaded. "Go back to Edgardale and send my mother or father back to help. Your face is really pale; you need to see a doctor. I'll be okay," she assured her.

Rhoda frowned heavily, but she accepted the reins and unsteadily mounted up. "Be careful, Ash. Don't do anything dangerous. I'll send your parents back to help." She gathered up the reins and turned for Edgardale.

Ashleigh squinted at where Aladdin had disappeared into the forest. She had wanted to help Rhoda get over her fear. But now it looked as though she and Stardust had just made things worse.

11

Ashleigh glanced at her watch. It was already six o'clock. There was much daylight left. She entered the woods, unsure which direction to take. There were two trails, and they both had so many hoofprints from rides she and Mona had taken that she couldn't tell which ones belonged to Aladdin. She followed a hunch and took the trail that led to the spring.

The spring was a fifteen-minute walk, but Ashleigh ran most of the way. When she entered the clearing, her lungs felt as though they were on fire. A loud snort alerted her that Aladdin was there. She smiled when she saw the colt standing a hundred yards away, nibbling on a small patch of grass, his reins dragging on the ground and his saddle still in place.

"Here, boy," Ashleigh coaxed as she slowly approached the colt. Aladdin took one more bite of grass, then blew through his nostrils and walked toward her.

"Whoa. Good boy," Ashleigh said as she reached out to grab his reins. She squatted down to run a hand over his legs. There were a few little scratches, but no lumps or hot spots.

She patted Aladdin's neck and heaved a sigh of relief. "You gave us quite a scare, running off like that. It's bad enough that Rhoda's hurt. What if you'd hurt yourself, too, and couldn't race?" Ashleigh frowned. The way things were, Aladdin probably wouldn't be running in the Derby anyway.

"Let's go," Ashleigh said as she set off down the trail. When they reached the clearing, she glanced at the lowering sun. They'd have to hurry if they wanted to make it back to Edgardale before sunset.

She clucked to Aladdin and jogged down the trail ahead of him, but after her earlier run, it didn't take long for Ashleigh to get tired. She stopped and rested with her hands on her knees, sucking in big gulps of air. Aladdin poked her with his nose, setting her off balance, and Ashleigh fell to her knees.

"Hey," she grouched as she got to her feet and dusted off her jeans. "I need to rest. I don't have four legs like you do."

Ashleigh rested for a minute while Aladdin cropped grass. As she studied the colt an idea popped into her head. She got up and checked the saddle. It was undamaged. She looked at her watch and again at the setting sun. They would make it home a lot quicker if she just got on Aladdin and rode him home.

The memory of the last time she had sneaked a ride on Aladdin popped into her head. She had fallen off, unable to control him. What if the same thing happened again? She sighed and tugged at Aladdin's reins. She would just have to keep walking back to the barn.

Ashleigh made it another quarter of a mile before she stopped again. Her riding boots were not made for this much walking. The seams cut into her ankles, and she could feel blisters forming. Aladdin was behaving so well. What could it hurt if she got on him and just walked him back to Edgardale? If he acted up, she could always get back off again.

She glanced around the field and spotted a large stump not too far off. She walked Aladdin to the stump and threw the reins over his head, climbing onto the makeshift mounting block. "You be good," she instructed the horse nervously. She put her foot in the stirrup and swung onto his broad back. "None of that running-away stuff."

Ashleigh paused when she touched down on the saddle. She looked at the ground. It was as far down as she had remembered. Her breath caught in her throat when Aladdin extended his nose, tugging on the reins, and began to walk.

After a few hundred feet Ashleigh began to relax.

Aladdin had already had his run. The big colt dropped his head and plodded along the trail like a stable horse. He was behaving perfectly, but Ashleigh stayed on her guard, knowing that it wouldn't take much to set him off again. She rocked to the sway of Aladdin's powerful stride, keeping her hands light on the reins, not wanting to transmit her excitement to Aladdin.

They walked for a mile without incident. Ashleigh's heart rose in her throat when a rabbit popped out of the bushes ten yards ahead, but Aladdin only flicked his ears. "Good boy." She reached down to pat him, wondering at the colt's calmness.

Maybe Aladdin did hurt himself, Ashleigh worried, *and that's why he's quiet.* He felt fine, but she knew that at a walk it was hard to tell if a horse was hurt.

Ashleigh clucked to Aladdin, and he broke into a brisk trot. Unprepared for his massive strides, Ashleigh was caught off balance and thrown back in the saddle. She pulled back on the reins, and immediately Aladdin slowed to a steady jog.

When Ashleigh's heartbeat had calmed down, she checked for unsoundness at the trot, but couldn't find any. Aladdin seemed to be traveling perfectly. *Too perfectly,* she thought.

Ashleigh wasn't as experienced as Rhoda. She knew Aladdin could get rid of her any time he wanted to.

But he hadn't spooked or tried to run away once.

Ashleigh smiled. She had wanted to get another rider on Aladdin to see if he would behave differently than he did with Rhoda. But she hadn't thought that *she* would be the rider. And her suspicions were correct! Aladdin was moving along the path as if he'd been going on trail rides all his life. The difference was that Ashleigh wasn't afraid.

Ashleigh's heart soared. Now all she had to do was find a way to keep Rhoda from being afraid!

Ashleigh pulled Aladdin back to a walk, her mind racing. At this point she didn't know how badly Rhoda was hurt, or even if she'd made it all the way back to Edgardale.

They were approaching the edge of the property line. Ashleigh was about to ask Aladdin to trot again when she saw a rider approaching. She pulled Aladdin to a halt and jumped to the ground, wincing when she landed hard on her feet. She didn't want to be caught riding Aladdin—she had been grounded for a week the last time.

Ashleigh began to lead the colt across the field once more when suddenly Aladdin froze in his tracks, his nostrils flaring, and trumpeted a loud whinny. "Easy, boy," Ashleigh said, holding tightly to the reins while Aladdin bowed his head and pranced around her.

Ashleigh heard the sound of hoofbeats and saw her

father coming down the trail at a full gallop on Stardust. He slowed the mare when he saw Aladdin dancing at the end of the reins.

"Ashleigh, are you all right?" Mr. Griffen pulled Stardust to a sliding stop and jumped from her back.

"We're fine," Ashleigh assured her father.

"Rhoda came back on Stardust and told us what happened," Mr. Griffen said as he traded horses with Ashleigh. "Your mother has taken her to the hospital." He looked sternly at Ashleigh. "You should have come back with Rhoda and let me go after Aladdin," he scolded.

Ashleigh looked up in surprise. "I couldn't come back without him. It was my fault he got loose— Stardust kicked at him."

Mr. Griffen squeezed Ashleigh's shoulder. "It's all right," he assured her. "Your mother and I probably would have done the same thing."

"Is Rhoda okay?" Ashleigh asked worriedly.

Mr. Griffen made a tsking sound and shook his head. "That cut on her head looked pretty nasty, but I don't think it was bad enough to need stitches. From the sound of things, Rhoda was lucky that she didn't break anything when she jumped."

He turned and inspected Aladdin. "The colt looks all right, but Mike and the vet are coming out to make sure," Mr. Griffen said as he turned toward Edgardale. "It's getting dark. Why don't you ride on ahead on

Stardust and let everyone know you're okay?"

When Ashleigh rode into the stable yard, everyone rushed out to greet her. "Aladdin's on the way," she said to Mike and the veterinarian. "I think he's all right."

"Here, Ash, let me take care of Stardust," Caroline offered as she took the reins from Ashleigh's hands.

"I'll help, too," Rory said.

"Thanks, guys," Ashleigh said gratefully, suddenly exhausted.

"Mom just called from the hospital to say that Rhoda is okay and they're on their way home," Caroline said. "She didn't even need stitches."

Ashleigh smiled. That was good news.

Mr. Griffen arrived with Aladdin, and Ashleigh went to see what the vet had to say. Mike stood watch over the big colt while the vet went over him inch by inch. After several long minutes the man stood and dusted his hands off. "Looks like everything is in order," he said. "This colt is tough. I'd give him a couple of days off, but I can't see any reason why he shouldn't run in the Derby on Saturday."

Everyone breathed a sigh of relief, except Ashleigh. She could think of one good reason why Aladdin couldn't run in the Derby: Rhoda. Ashleigh had to convince the jockey that Aladdin wasn't a bad horse—she just needed to trust him and ride him with confidence.

Ashleigh walked back to the house to wait for Rhoda. She climbed the stairs to her room and pulled off her boots, then stretched out on her bed. She hadn't realized she'd drifted off to sleep until the bedroom door creaked and Rhoda came in.

"Hey there," Rhoda said as she sat gingerly on the bed. "How are you doing? Did everything go okay?"

Ashleigh sat up in bed and smiled. "Yeah. The vet said Aladdin needs to take a few days off, but he's cleared to run in the Derby. What about you? Do you feel well enough to ride?"

Rhoda frowned. "Yeah, I guess I have to. But I don't know how much good it will do. Mike talked to Mr. Danworth, and they'll make a decision after Aladdin's next work, on Thursday. If he doesn't go well, that's the end of it, Ash," Rhoda said, shaking her head.

Ashleigh looked at the horse calendar by her bed. She had only a couple more days to figure out how to make that ride perfect. If she could keep Rhoda from worrying about Aladdin's behavior when she was riding him, then maybe he would settle down for her. *But how?* Ashleigh wondered desperately.

Rhoda lay back on the bed and closed her eyes, then she groaned.

"Does your head hurt?" Ashleigh asked. "Do you want an aspirin?"

"It's not that." Rhoda waved her hand in the air as if

trying to erase something. "Every time I close my eyes, all I can see is that big drop ... that Jessica's Jump. I never want to see that thing again!"

Ashleigh sat straight up in bed. *That's it!* She had the solution! She scrambled off the bed, almost tripping when her foot got tangled in the bedspread.

"What's the matter?" Rhoda sat up in alarm.

"Nothing," Ashleigh said, opening the bedroom door. "You get some sleep. I'll see you in the morning." She ran down the hall to call Mona.

"Do you really think your plan will work?" Mona said when Ashleigh gave her the details.

"It's got to," Ashleigh said. "Rhoda needs to see that Aladdin will go well for her if she's not worrying about him acting up. The only way to do that is to distract her, and Jessica's Jump is the one thing that really gets her attention."

"I don't know, Ash." Mona's voice was full of doubt. "There are a lot of people around your place. Aladdin isn't supposed to go out until Thursday. How are you going to get Rhoda to ride him before then?"

Ashleigh frowned. She didn't know how she was going to pull it off, but something would work out. Her mother and Caroline were going dress shopping on Wednesday after school. Caro had already bought Ashleigh a dress for her birthday, so she wouldn't be expected to go. Now all she had to do was figure a way around her father, Jonas, and Rory.

"Don't worry," Ashleigh said. "Just be ready on Wednesday."

When Ashleigh and Mona hopped off the school bus on Wednesday afternoon, Ashleigh had a stomach-ache. If her plan didn't work, that would be the end of the Derby for Aladdin.

The Danworths would be there the next day to watch Aladdin breeze. Ashleigh had no doubt about how the colt would perform if Rhoda didn't have her confidence back, and they would scratch him from the race for sure.

She couldn't let that happen.

"See you soon," she said to Mona as they parted at the end of the driveway.

Ashleigh hurried to the house to change her clothes. She was pleased to find Rhoda sleeping soundly when she entered the bedroom. Ashleigh began the first stages of her plan, setting the alarm clock and leaving Rhoda a note on the dresser. She slipped out of the house and down to the barn to start on her stalls. Twenty minutes later she heard footfalls coming up the aisle.

"Rory and I are heading to the feed store," Mr. Griffen said as he stopped in front of the stall Ash-leigh was cleaning. "We'll be gone about an hour and a half."

Rory followed their father with Ashleigh's kitten tucked under his arm. "We're going to get some ice cream, too," Mr. Griffen added. "Your mother and Caroline are heading into town to pick up Caroline's dress," he said to Ashleigh. "Jonas is here if you need anything, and Rhoda is upstairs taking a nap. Will you be okay for a couple of hours?"

Ashleigh grabbed the wheelbarrow and continued down the aisle. "Sure, I'll be fine. Mona will be here soon to go for a ride." She waved good-bye to them, then emptied the wheelbarrow and ran to call Mona. "It's time," she said. "Everyone's going into town. Get over here right now!" She hung up the barn phone and raced to saddle Stardust. She was just tightening the girth when Mona arrived.

"Wow, this place is quiet," Mona said. "Where did everybody go?"

"Rhoda is sleeping, and I think Jonas might be taking a nap, too. I haven't seen him for a while. Everyone else is in town," Ashleigh said as she grabbed Aladdin's halter and called him in from the paddock. She closed Aladdin in his stall so he'd be easier for Rhoda to catch, then went to the tack room to pull out his saddle and bridle.

"You don't think Rhoda will be suspicious that all this stuff is just lying here?" Mona said.

Ashleigh grinned. "I'm hoping she's going to be so worried when she sees my note that she won't think— she'll just get on Aladdin and ride like the wind!"

Ashleigh unsnapped Stardust from the crossties and led her out of the barn.

"What if Rhoda doesn't find the note?" Mona asked. They mounted up and turned the two mares down the trail.

"She'll find it," Ashleigh said, her voice sounding more confident than she felt.

"What did you write?"

Ashleigh grinned. "I said I needed to do more research for a jumping paper I was working on for my next speech, so I was going to the creek to see how far across I could jump."

Mona laughed and slapped Ashleigh a high five. "If that doesn't get her, nothing will."

Ashleigh pointed to a tree at the edge of the field. "You wait over there. When you see Rhoda coming, wave to me."

Ashleigh walked Stardust up and down and waited. Her hands shook on the reins as the minutes passed and Stardust began to fidget.

She walked the mare to the edge of Jessica's Jump and stared down into the rocky bottom. Poor Jessica.

It must have been terrifying when the girl realized that she wasn't going to make it all the way across.

A shiver ran up Ashleigh's back. Stardust shifted her weight, and several small rocks rolled from their place on the edge of the creek bank and rattled down, making a splash in the shallow water. Stardust snorted and backed away, and Ashleigh reached down to pat her neck, glancing across the field to where Mona was waiting. There was still no sign of Rhoda.

After another five minutes Ashleigh got the signal she was waiting for—Mona's arm waving.

"Come on, girl," she said to Stardust. "We've got a couple of careers to save." She asked Stardust for a canter and began a wide circle, as though she were setting up for a jump. She tried to hide her excited smile when she saw Rhoda racing across the field on Aladdin, her body low and her face set in determination.

"Ashleigh, wait!" Rhoda called as she slapped Aladdin with the reins, trying to get more speed.

Ashleigh pretended not to see the jockey. She cantered Stardust out of the circle and headed straight for the creek. It felt like forever as she waited for Rhoda to get close enough for Ashleigh to pretend that she had just noticed her. She didn't want to give away their ruse by turning to look.

The creek loomed closer and closer, and Ashleigh was beginning to think she might actually have to jump it when Rhoda pulled up beside her and grabbed one of her reins.

Ashleigh put on a look of total surprise when Rhoda stood in the stirrups and brought them to a halt at the edge of the creek.

"Are you crazy?" Rhoda yelled as she jumped off Aladdin and pulled the reins from Ashleigh's hands. "Do you want to end up in the hospital? I was worried sick that I wouldn't get here in time and I'd have to pick you up from the bottom of the creek."

"I just wanted to do some more research for my school paper," Ashleigh said innocently.

Rhoda pulled the reins over Stardust's head, her hands shaking as she did so. She mounted up on Aladdin. "I'm ponying you home," Rhoda said with a frown. "And I haven't made up my mind yet if I'm going to tell your parents or not."

Ashleigh bit her lip to keep from grinning. Her plan was working perfectly—except for the part about telling her parents. Rhoda was fuming, but she had forgotten all about her fear of riding Aladdin, and sat him like the great equestrian she was.

"What are you smiling about?" Rhoda grouched as she nudged Aladdin into a trot.

"Nothing," Ashleigh said. Just then she saw Mona hiding in the cover of the woods. She gave Mona a thumbs-up sign when Rhoda wasn't looking.

Rhoda studied Ashleigh's face. "This isn't a laughing matter," she said, her voice full of suspicion.

Ashleigh broke into a wide grin. "Look at you," she said. "You just rode Aladdin like you were coming down the homestretch in the Kentucky Derby, and he went perfectly. He hasn't spooked once!"

Rhoda paused, her eyes widening when she realized that what Ashleigh had said was true.

"You can do it," Ashleigh said. "You can ride Aladdin in the Kentucky Derby!"

Rhoda turned to Ashleigh, her face stern. "So you planned all of this, you sneaky devil? I might have guessed," she scolded. "I still might tell your parents." But she couldn't hold the frown any longer, and a large smile broke through. "Though I have to say, I'm glad you did it."

Rhoda gave Ashleigh back her reins, then asked Aladdin for a canter. "I had forgotten how good it felt to ride this horse for fun," Rhoda said with a smile.

Ashleigh clucked Stardust into a canter, too. They had to get the horses home and back in their stalls before Jonas found out or her family came home. Riding side by side, their horses' strides smooth and easy, the girls smiled at each other. There were only three days left until the Derby, and for the first time in a long time, it looked as though there was hope!

12

The Danworths were already at the barn when Ashleigh stepped off the school bus on Thursday afternoon.

"Hey, Ash." Thirteen-year-old Peter Danworth waved hello as Ashleigh walked into the stable. "Looks like you've been taking good care of my horse."

Ashleigh smiled. Aladdin stood in the crossties, saddled and ready to go. Rhoda was scratching his ears, and the colt had his head tilted to one side, loving every minute of it.

"We're all ready to go," Mike said. "The Wortons are expecting us."

"I've got to run up to the house and change," Ashleigh said, indicating the clean jeans she had worn to school.

Mrs. Griffen handed Ashleigh Stardust's reins. "I think we can let it go this once, Ash. Everyone's ready.

Let's not keep the Danworths waiting."

Mr. Griffen herded everyone out the barn door. "We'll drive over and meet you girls at the track."

Ashleigh led Stardust out the door and mounted up, waiting for Aladdin to ride beside her so she could slide the pony strap through his bit. Aladdin approached, and Stardust started to lay her ears back. "No way," she said as she gave Stardust a little slap. "Not again." Stardust bobbed her head and her ears flicked back and forth as she listened to the sound of Ashleigh's voice.

She slipped the pony strap on Aladdin and they trotted toward the Wortons'. "How do you feel?" Ashleigh asked Rhoda. "Are you nervous?"

Rhoda shrugged and reached forward to pat Aladdin on the shoulder. "Yes, I'm a little nervous, but I'm always that way when I'm ready to win a big race."

That's more like it, Ashleigh thought.

When they reached the track, Ashleigh let Aladdin go at the entrance gate. The jockey had instructions to breeze Aladdin a light half mile. It was up to Rhoda and Aladdin now. The fate of the Derby rested with them.

Ashleigh rode Stardust over to where her family and the Danworths were standing next to Mike and dismounted.

"My dad says Aladdin has really been acting up and he might have to scratch him from the Derby," Peter said nervously. "But he looks like he's going fine now."

"I think we might have solved the problem," Ashleigh said confidently. She leaned against the rail, watching as Rhoda and Aladdin approached the half-mile pole. Aladdin's ears flicked back and forth, waiting for his rider's cue. When Rhoda asked him to run, the big colt stretched his neck out and got down to business. Ashleigh saw his ears twitch at the black-and-white striped eighth pole, but that was the only indication that his mind wasn't 100 percent on his work.

Mike clicked the stopwatch as Aladdin crossed the finish line. "Forty-seven and change," he announced, his eyes wide with amazement. He handed the clock to Mr. Danworth. "That's a pretty fast clip for a horse that was only breezing. What do you say?"

Mr. Danworth and his wife looked at the stopwatch, then up at Aladdin as Rhoda galloped him steadily around the turn and slowed him to a trot. Everyone held their breath, waiting for Mr. Danworth to speak.

"I'd say we're going to the Derby!" Mr. Danworth said, and twirled his wife in a little dance spin.

Everyone cheered, but Ashleigh cheered the loudest. Aladdin and Rhoda were going to the Derby!

Mrs. Griffen pulled Ashleigh aside. "Aladdin sure worked well today," she said, raising her eyebrows.

Ashleigh nodded cautiously. She could tell by the sly look on her mother's face that she knew more than Ashleigh had wanted her to.

Mrs. Griffen handed Ashleigh a crumpled piece of paper, and Ashleigh gulped when she recognized the note she had left for Rhoda.

"I don't suppose this note has anything to do with Aladdin training so well today, does it?" Mrs. Griffen asked.

Ashleigh looked down at the ground and nodded.

"I should have known," Mrs. Griffen said, shaking her head. "At some point I want to hear all about this, Ashleigh. But there's no way I can ground you from the Kentucky Derby. Let's just wait till *after* Aladdin wins."

Peter snaked his hand around, giving Ashleigh a high five. "I knew you'd do something to save the day!"

Ashleigh laughed, relieved not to be in trouble, and practically shaking with excitement.

On Saturday Aladdin would show them all!

"He looks like a girl," Peter said when he saw all the red roses Ashleigh and Caroline had woven into Aladdin's mane and tail.

Ashleigh smiled. "He's going to have a whole blanket of these to match when the race is over," Ashleigh said, referring to the blanket of roses that was given to the winner of the Kentucky Derby.

The paddock judge called the riders to the saddling ring, and Ashleigh waved to Rhoda as she stepped from the jockey's quarters. She looked great in the Danworths' black-and-red racing silks. But most important, Rhoda's chin was up and she looked confident.

The jockeys were given a leg up, and the crowd scrambled to the front rail at the sound of the bugle calling the horses to the post. The attendance for this running of the Kentucky Derby was a record breaker, and Ashleigh had to squeeze through the throng of people that crowded in front of the white spired grandstands.

"Over here." She motioned to the others, grabbing Mona's and Peter's hands and dragging them through the crush of racing fans. She glanced back and saw Caroline, all dressed up, following them.

"Don't you want to sit up in the Danworths' box, Caro?" Ashleigh called to her sister.

"Not today." Caroline beamed, holding her fancy hat to keep it from falling off. "I want to be down at the rail where the action is."

Ashleigh grinned at her sister and led the way.

The crowd quieted to a hush and stood at attention when the announcer called for the playing of "My Old Kentucky Home." As the music played, the Derby entries paraded onto the track led by their pony horses.

Ashleigh could hardly believe that Edgardale had a horse in the Derby! How many times had she watched this race on television, dreaming of the day one of their horses would run in this race? She felt tears come to her eyes as the voices of the fans sang the words to "My Old Kentucky Home."

When the song was finished, the crowd roared their appreciation. Ashleigh stood on tiptoe, squinting to find Aladdin in the post parade.

The black colt's ears were pricked and he danced nervously as the fans leaned over the fence, waving their racing programs and shouting encouragement to the jockeys. Ashleigh smiled proudly as Stardust, with Mike's regular pony boy aboard, stepped smartly down the track, her head held high.

Ashleigh wished she were old enough to pony Aladdin herself, but it would be five more years until she was eligible.

"Stardust looks great, Ash," Mona said. "I think she's helping to keep Aladdin calm."

Peter pointed to the tote board, where the odds were tallied. "Looks like he's going off at pretty high odds again."

Ashleigh shrugged. Aladdin had won at high odds before. He could do it again.

Caroline squeezed her hand. "Don't let that bother you, Ash. He can do it," she said confidently.

A commotion broke out, and several people near Ashleigh pointed down the track. Star Gazer had broken loose from his handler and was running sideways down the track. Zach Jackson cocked the colt's head to one side to keep him from running away. The outrider came to the rescue, but not before Star Gazer bumped into Aladdin and Stardust, unsettling the black colt. Aladdin stepped sideways and chomped nervously at the bit.

"Hang on to him, Rhoda," Ashleigh whispered as the pony rider nudged Stardust forward and pulled Aladdin to the side to calm him down.

Rhoda gave them a thumbs-up sign when they trotted past on their way to the starting gate, but Ashleigh thought her smile looked a little crooked. She took a deep breath and hoped for the best.

Tom Vargas, Star Gazer's trainer, stepped up to the fence nearby. "He just wanted to take a victory lap before the race," he commented with a laugh, and slapped the man next to him on the back.

Ashleigh glared at him. He wouldn't be laughing when this race was over and Aladdin had proven once and for all that he was the faster horse.

"The horses are approaching the starting gate for the running of the one hundred and twenty-fifth Kentucky Derby," the announcer said. "Please get your wagers in early to avoid being shut out at the window."

Ashleigh watched intently as the horses began to load into the gate. The race was a mile and a quarter. The horses would break from the gate, passing in front of the grandstand, then circle the track and come back to the finish line in front of the grandstand once more. Aladdin had drawn the eighth position in a sixteen-horse field and stood quietly next to Stardust, waiting to walk into the gate.

"Number one, Fancy Flight, has been loaded," the announcer called as the gate crew began to lead the horses in one by one. "Young Dubliner is in, and the number six and seven horses are waiting."

There was a long pause as Ashleigh waited for the man to call Aladdin's name. "What are they waiting for?" she asked Peter.

Peter stood on his toes. "I think there's a rider off behind the gate." He leaned forward and squinted. "It looks like it might be Rhoda."

Ashleigh's stomach dropped. Had Rhoda lost her nerve?

"Aladdin's Treasure is being delayed at the gate," the deep voice boomed over the loudspeaker.

Ashleigh grabbed the railing to steady herself. Rhoda couldn't back out now. They were at the gate. The race was about to start!

A murmur rippled through the crowd. Ashleigh heard bits and pieces of conversation, but nothing to tell her what was happening. Her heart pounded hard in her chest. *What's happening?* she wondered desperately.

"Looks like she's back in the saddle." Peter breathed a sigh of relief.

"Yes!" Ashleigh shouted, and banged her fist on the rail.

Mike joined them at the rail. "The rest of your family is up in the clubhouse with the Danworths," he said to Ashleigh. "That was quite a scare there a moment ago."

"What happened?" Ashleigh asked, keeping her eyes glued on the starting gate.

Mike shifted to get a better view. "One of the security guards said the number nine horse took a kick at Aladdin. The track vet wanted to make sure he hadn't gotten hit."

Ashleigh felt a rush of relief. As long as the interruption hadn't upset Rhoda, everything would be fine.

"The horses are all loaded," the announcer called. The crowd waited tensely for the ringing of the bell that would signal the start of the race. "And they're off! Aladdin's Treasure breaks out first, with Flying Fury challenging him for the lead."

"What's Aladdin doing out on the lead?" Ashleigh cried in shock, but before they crossed the finish line for the first time, Rhoda had pulled the colt back to the middle of the pack.

Aladdin's neck was bowed as he fought the pressure on the bit, but the jockey held him to his position. Was Rhoda afraid to let him run?

"He's not a front-running horse," Mike said. "Rhoda's saving him for his stretch run."

Ashleigh watched as the horses came out of the turn and headed down the backstretch, Aladdin barely visible in the middle of the group. She hoped Mike was right.

"Young Dubliner moves into third, with Star Gazer coming up to take fourth place on the inside rail," the announcer said. "Aladdin's Treasure is making a big move on the inside, coming into fifth behind Star Gazer."

"Isn't he moving a little too early?" Peter asked as he squeezed in next to Ashleigh. "What if he runs out of steam?"

Mike was silent, and Ashleigh could tell from the look on his face that he was as puzzled as the rest of them. *Why would Rhoda want him next to Star Gazer? She knows that colt is trouble,* Ashleigh thought.

The loudspeaker crackled as the excited voice of the announcer continued the call. "As the horses come out of the final turn, Fancy Flight is fading, and Star Gazer moves into position to take the lead. Aladdin's Treasure is hemmed in on the inside rail, and Raider's Silhouette makes a bold move from the middle of the track."

"He's stuck on the rail!" Ashleigh screamed, trying to be heard over the roar of the crowd. "What's she doing?"

The horses came out of the turn, pounding down the homestretch.

"And down the stretch they come!" the announcer called. "Raider's Silhouette passes Star Gazer in the center of the track and moves into second as Young Dubliner tries to hold off the challenge."

Ashleigh strained her eyes to follow Aladdin on the inside rail, but Star Gazer blocked her view. With a sixteenth of a mile to go, the little bay colt looked as though he was angry at being passed by another horse, and he moved off the rail to make an assault on Raider's Silhouette.

Ashleigh saw the hole open up and held her breath. Would Rhoda go for it? Time seemed to stand still, and then the jockey lifted her whip and Aladdin shot through the hole, gaining ground on Star Gazer and moving on to pass him.

"It's Star Gazer, Raider's Silhouette, and Aladdin's Treasure in a three-way battle for the lead!" the announcer said as the crowd went crazy. "They're down to the wire, and Aladdin's Treasure pulls ahead by a nose. Star Gazer battles to hold off the challenge from Raider's Silhouette!"

"Come on, Aladdin!" Ashleigh screamed with Mona, Peter, and Caroline as the horses approached the finish line.

Rhoda scrubbed the reins up and down Aladdin's

neck, turning her head to see how close the other horses were. Aladdin gave her his all, pinning his ears and pounding the dirt as they crossed the wire half a length in front of Star Gazer.

"He did it!" Ashleigh screamed as she hugged Peter, then jumped up and down clutching Mona's and Caroline's hands. "Aladdin won the Kentucky Derby!"

Caroline threw her fancy hat in the air and it tumbled over the crowd.

"You'll never get it back," Ashleigh said, laughing, as she watched another Derby fan pick it up and wave it like a flag.

"Who cares?" Caroline yelled. "We just won the Kentucky Derby!"

"Everyone down into the winner's circle," Mike said excitedly as he herded them toward the gate to meet Aladdin and Rhoda.

Star Gazer's trainer passed by as Ashleigh stepped into the winner's circle. He caught her eye and looked away in disgust, shaking his head.

Ashleigh resisted the urge to stick her tongue out at the man. Aladdin had beat Star Gazer fair and square, and everyone there knew it.

Aladdin trotted back to the finish line to the roar of the crowd and flashing cameras. Rhoda flagged her whip to the stewards and waved to the racing fans.

Mike walked out to hold Aladdin still while the

Danworths and Griffens took their places in the winner's circle. When everyone was set, he led the colt in and the blanket of roses was placed over Aladdin's withers.

"Peter," Mike called, yelling to be heard above the noise of the crowd, "this is your horse. Why don't you take Aladdin's reins for the win photo?"

Peter took hold of Aladdin's reins, then motioned for Ashleigh to join him, handing her one of the reins as she stepped to his side.

Ashleigh looked at him questioningly, but Peter nudged her, grinning. "I don't know what you did, Ash, but I'm sure you're behind all of this," he said cheerfully.

Ashleigh laughed and reached up to stroke Aladdin's forehead. "Maybe I'll tell you about it sometime," she said. But all she wanted at that moment was for Rhoda and Aladdin to revel in their victory.

Mrs. Griffen stepped forward and tucked a lock of hair behind Ashleigh's ear, smoothing it for the picture.

"Everyone ready?" the track photographer said.

Ashleigh turned Aladdin's head to face the camera and smiled up at Rhoda.

Rhoda plucked a rose and passed it down to Ashleigh. "Happy late birthday, Ash."

Ashleigh blinked as the camera flashed. This was a birthday she would never forget!

CHRIS PLATT rode her first pony when she was two years old and hasn't been without a horse since. Chris spent five years at racetracks throughout Oregon, working as an exercise rider, jockey, and assistant trainer. She currently lives in Reno, Nevada, with her husband, Brad, five horses, three cats, a llama, a pot-bellied pig, and a parrot. Between books, Chris rides endurance horses for a living, and drives draft horses for fun in her spare time.